The Whispering Forest

Christopher Young

Table of Contents

Prologue...4

Chapter One The Edge of the Trees.........................5

Chapter Two The Hidden Spark............................11

Chapter Three Wands, Warnings, and Wandering Mushrooms..............17

Chapter Four Fire and Fog...................................28

Chapter Five The Map That Shouldn't Exist.........35

Chapter Six The Shatterspires.............................41

Chapter Seven The Plateau's Shadow...................46

Chapter Eight Fire in the East.............................53

Chapter Nine The Hollow Map............................61

Chapter Ten The Watchers of the East.................66

Chapter Eleven Into the Plateau..........................71

Chapter Twelve The Tower of Threads..................77

Chapter Thirteen The Cost of Magic....................92

Chapter Fourteen Return of the Whispering Forest.................97

Epilogue The Forest Remembers.........................105

Prologue

The Eastern Plateau had been a legend once a land behind the Cracked Mountains that was impossible to approach. But, when clouds darkened and dragons did not fly, a new nation descended from the fog, with fire that clung to sky and soil like a fever, and with curses that etched themselves into the bones of the land... The common folk fought well. But they had steel swords, and the magic of the Plateau was old. Among the soldiers sent to the frontlines was a reserved man named Callen, father to a youth who would soon wander into a secret long hidden under moss and moonlight. Callen had never believed in prophecies. But as he marched toward the fog, he felt like a page in someone else's story.

The Edge of the Trees

Everyone in Elder Hollow was aware of avoiding the Whispering Forest.

Not because the trees stood too close together, all in a row, like crones whispering in the dark, or the way the wind blew through their thick, knotted limbs always sounded deep, as if, whispering someone's name. No—the real reason was the stories. The ones that didn't end their story in the shape of "happily ever after," but rather ended with "and no one ever saw them again."

Elric knew the stories. He'd heard them a thousand times, usually while he stood on his head or tried to levitate stones with his mind.

He also knew that, despite all rumors and warnings, no one had ever gone in for nearly half a century.

Which is why, when his runaway book scampered toward the forest edge on a sunny mid-morning, Elric did one thing that every grown-up in Elder Hollow would say not to do.

He followed it.

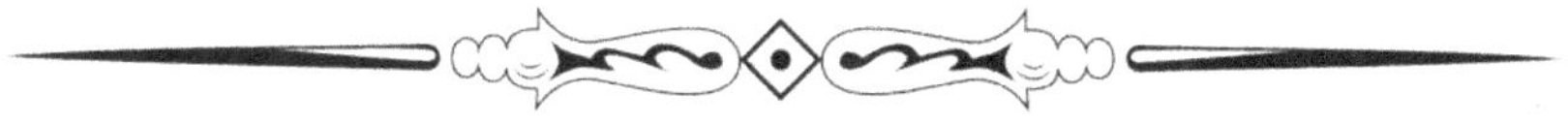

"Stop!" he hissed, ducking under a branch and hopping over a root. "You're not even supposed to have legs!"

The book—a red leather-bound small one called Beginner Charms and Other Things That Go Boom—opened wide as it went, its parchment pages beating wildly like wings. It had grown legs after Elric, drowsy at breakfast, had accidentally cast a walking spell meant for boots.

It ran straight into the trees, and Elric was determined to catch it before anyone noticed.

As Elric passed the decaying stone arch that marked the edge of mapped woods, air changed. Not just cooler—but fuller, thicker, like hushed anticipation before a grand symphony. Trees rose higher here, their trunks scored with white, glowing light, as if they were pipes delivering the forest breath. Leaves rustled not with wind, but with understanding. Vines twisted partly in his direction. A flower turned its face toward him.

The forest hadn't just accepted him.

It had been waiting for long.

The moment his foot crossed the line, a stillness waved out a silent breath, as though the entire glade had waited until now for air. Shadows parted a little. A root curled out, dusted in moss, and far away, a single silver bell rang—quiet, distant, and impossible.

Elric blinked. The forest was awake.

And somehow, it recognized his name.

Elric's pace slowed, brushing away a branch that dropped one pale greenish leaf into his hair. He looked up. The canopy above him glowed with a soft greenish hue, like moonlight through water in a pond.

The book stopped.

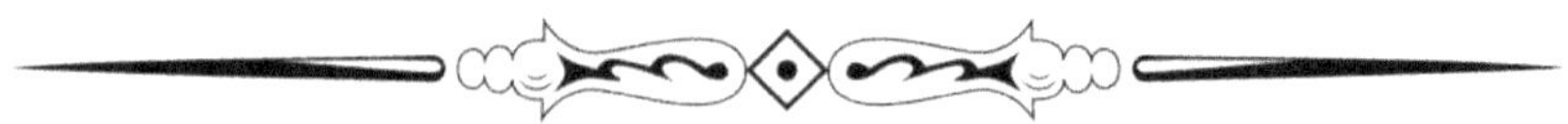

It crouched in a small clearing, panting. (Elric had no clue how or why it would pant, but it was making panting sounds.)

"You," Elric growled, moving forward. "Are so grounded."

When he moved to pick it up, he heard a rustling behind him, and he instantly spun around.

Nothing.

It was nothing but a cloud of golden pollen suspended in the air, drifting slowly past.

When he spun around again, the book was gone.

"No, no, no—come on!" he moaned, spinning in circles. "Where'd you—

A soft voice, barely above a whisper, spoke softly in his ear:

"Erratic…"

He tensed.

"Hello?" he croaked, his voice cracking.

Silence.

The leaves rustling and the distant thrum of magic lingering in the air.

And then, to his surprise, the ground beneath him started to glow.

Elric sprang back as a jarring thrum vibrated through the ground below—took a deep, shaken breath, realizing it wasn't an earthquake, but a heartbeat. A vortex of blazing runes erupted at his feet, etching a perfect circle into the mossy earth in light so blinding it stole his breath. The runes weren't static—quivered and changed, twisting like water-coated silver ink, re-forming themselves as if they thought.

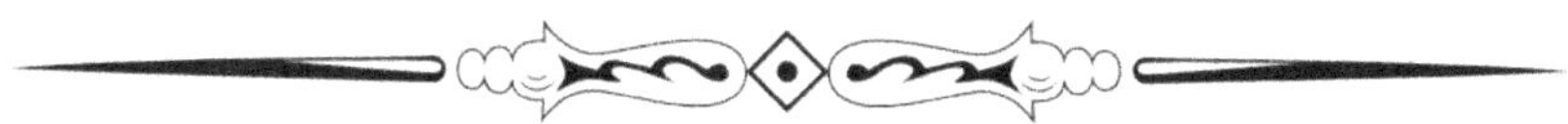

He tried to move, but air turned as sticky as honey in his legs. The runes rose from his hand—inches at first—drifting like on unseen glass. They whirred slowly, singing, a low chime that tickled his teeth.

Each symbol pulsed with a shifting color—one gold molten, another frost blue, another dark red of coals in blackness. As Elric watched, they began to fade—not into the ground, but into being itself, as if folding across planes. They faded away one by one with soft, wet breaths, like ice to fire.

He felt them on his flesh as they disappeared—not exactly pain, but heat and memory. Brushings of old dreams.

A final rune hung at eye level. It seemed stuck there, suspended in mid-air, and then flickered. Once.

And disappeared.

The forest exhaled.

Elric collapsed backward, his heart racing. The circle where the runes had danced was vacant—no scorch marks, no trace. Only a faint smell of lightning and lavender lingered.

Elric, did what any sane, not-at-all-prepared-for-this twelve-year-old would do.

He smiled.

"Cool."

Elric slouched over and placed his hand on where the glowing runes had vanished. The moss still buzzed. Humming. A fizzy can of soda against his fingertips.

Real magic.

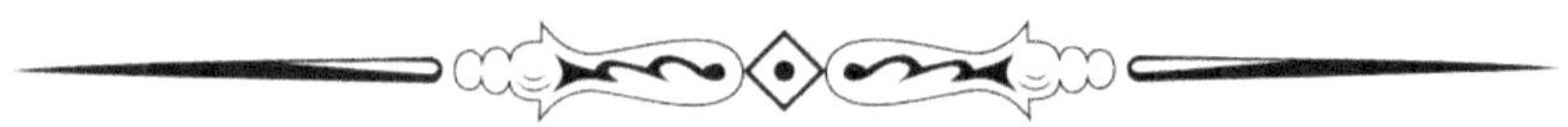

Not the half-thought-throughs from the back of an old book or botched spells gone wrong that had caused socks to disappear (he still hadn't found them). This was crazy—old, alive, observing him.

"Erratic…" the voice whispered again, this time just a bit more anxious.

"I heard you already," he said to them, glancing around. "Where are you?"

"Behind you."

Elric sprang a foot off the ground and turned around.

Nothing.

Then something fluffy dropped off a branch above and landed on his head with a thud.

"Ack! What the—" He flailed and tried to grab the fuzzy creature now stuck to his hair. He yanked it loose and held it away from him.

It blinked at him with enormous golden eyes, its tail thumping back and forth like a cat pondering a shoelace. The creature had rabbit ears long and tufted, dragonfly wings that buzzed when it sneezed, and an acorn helmet the size of a nut lopsidedly perched on its head.

"Elric of Elder Hollow," it squeaked in a deeper-than-hoped-for voice.

"You have trespassed, trod upon ancient glyphs, and awakened the Forest watch. What do you have to say for yourself?"

"I was after a book," Elric confessed.

The creature tilted its head. "A book."

"Yeah. Legs. Red cover." "Highly fast."

The creature sniffed. "Hmm. That makes sense."

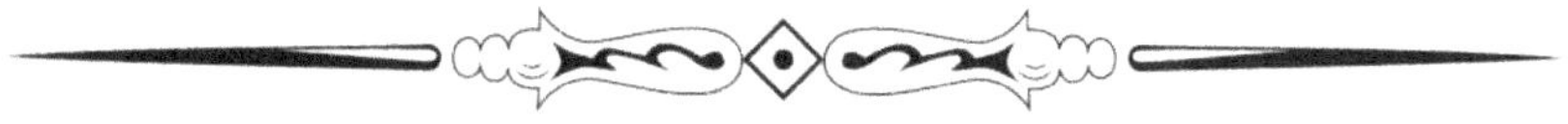

It leapt from his palms onto a surrounding boulder. "Name's Nib. Forest Guide, First Class. Small Secrets Keeper and Sandwich Supreme Eater."

"You're a sandwich eater?"

"Only the best. Peanut butter and more jam, mostly."

Elric scrunched up his face.

Nib didn't hear him. "You walked over a Memory Circle. You escaped lightly. You didn't cry and lose your name. The forest does not like to be walked upon, but this is uncommon."

"But it showed me something," Elric said quietly. "A symbol… it felt like it wanted me to see it."

Nib's wings buzzed thoughtfully. "Well, well. Maybe, it did. Or maybe it just thinks you're snack sized."

Elric looked down at the faint shimmer still clinging to his boots. "What happens now?"

Nib stared at him. "Now? Now, since you're involved. The forest's left a smell on you, boy. You've brushed the curtain. You've ignited the flame."

He darted back onto Elric's shoulder, lighter than he'd thought. "You're not leaving like you entered. That's for certain."

A shiver ran through Elric's spine.

And somewhere deeper into the forest, something began to howl.

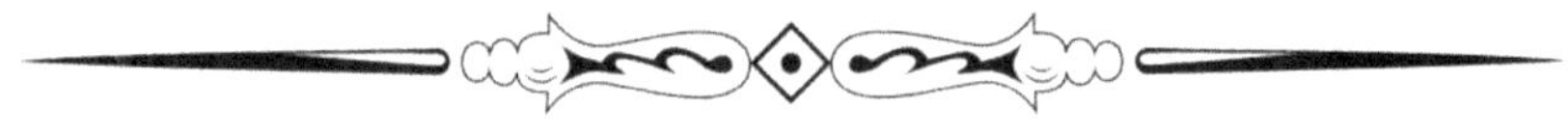

Chapter Two
The Hidden Spark

Elric had always hoped that when magic actually happens, the world would twinkle. Bells would ring. Stars would flash. Some stranger would hand you a glowing staff and declare you to be a chosen one.

But, as he walked with Nib into the forest, none of this happened.

Instead, his boots squelched in the mud. He tripped over roots. A plum-sized beetle buzzed into his ear and tried to stay.

Still—behind the crammed, mossy messiness, Elric felt something. As if his bones were singing a song they hadn't remembered they knew.

Nib fluttered just ahead, occasionally turning to make sure Elric wasn't being eaten by anything. "You're lucky it was me who found you," the creature said. "Could've been a gloomshade. Or worse. There's a vine beast out here that thinks everything's a sandwich."

"How comforting," Elric muttered.

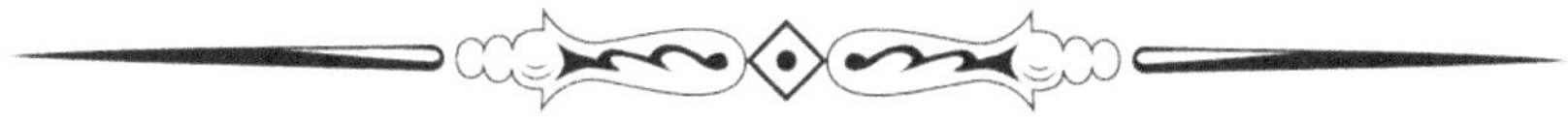

The path wound underfoot, no longer a path but a suggestion. Trees leaned overhead, barking furrowed like fists. Leaves whispered in tongues Elric did not speak.

"Where are we going?" he said, swatting aside a branch that immediately slapped him in the face.

Nib pointed with his tail. "To the Glimmer well. It's where the woods reveal truths to you."

"Such as, what truths?"

"Magic ones. Dangerous ones. Unique one, one that catches your attention instantly."

Elric's eyes widened. "Me?"

Nib turned around, hovering. "Don't act so innocent. You actually believe runes like those just show up for anyone who comes in here with crazy spell books?"

Elric looked down at his feet, then his hands. He didn't feel magical. He felt like a dirtier version of himself with a squirrel-fairy giving him missions.

Still. his fingers tingled.

After another patch of thorny silence, the trees suddenly parted.

They entered a hollow where the trees parted in a cathedral ring, their twisted trunks inclining up above like vaulted roofs. Sunlight poured through the canopy in splintered shafts of gold, cutting across the drifting mist like holy light through stained glass.

"The Glimmer well," Nib announced, grandly waving a paw.

In the middle of the clearing stood a pool that shone—glass-silken and motionless, as if time itself did not dare to break its stillness. It

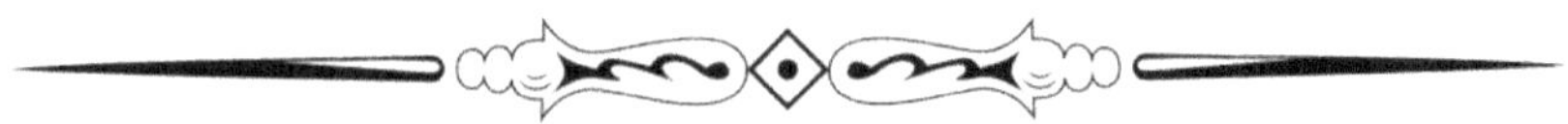

radiated a gentle light, not from any reflection of the sun, but from an inner quiet enchantment: gold and blue throbbed glimmered under the water's surface, like the pulsing of a dreaming heartbeat.

Crystals jutted out of the white, thin mossy banks, their points trilling softly in a harmony that vibrated in Elric's marrow. The melodies weren't anything like music, but they echoed deep inside him—like the forest was singing without sound.

Above, a cloud of floating lights danced in lazy whirls. They resembled fireflies at first, but as they whirled closer, Elric saw they were insect seeds or stars or maybe both, flowing on the winds that didn't exist. They left a pale shimmer, a filament of silver or purple mist, behind them before they vanished, leaving a tenuous spiral that shattered away into nothing.

The air had a different scent here—acrid, like frost-nipped apples and rain on stones. Lilac and wood smoke filled the air, and the silence wasn't empty, it was listening. As though the entire grove was holding its breath.

Elric stepped forward, catching his breath. "It's beautiful…"

"It's old," Nib said. "Older than any magic you've ever heard of. It reveals what's hidden within. Dip in the water, and the forest reveals to you what you are."

Elric knelt on the ground beside the pool and felt the warmth radiating from it, but his fingers didn't touch water. His reflection blinked up at him, and beneath that something else shone in the depths—a glint of another face, an older, tired one, watching.

"Nib." Elric breathed, not wanting to turn away. "Do you see that?"

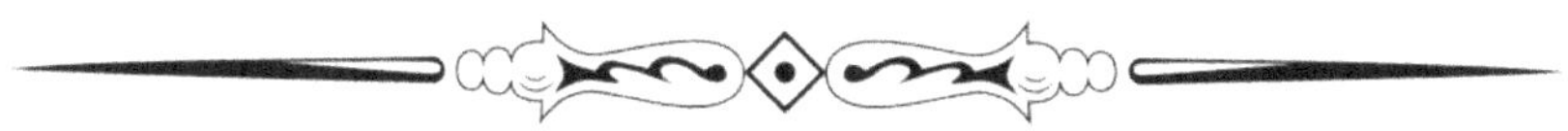

Nib crept forward slowly, humming wings. "Yup. And I hope to be able to stand it if it blinks next."

Gulping, Elric extended his hand. The water surged at his fingertips.

As soon as his hand broke it, it happened.

A sudden heat flashed along Elric's arm, the instant his fingers brushed against the edge of the pool. Not fire-heated warmth—but something ancient, like sunlight trapped in amber, suddenly released. He drew a breath as the heat poured through his veins, pouring toward his heart.

The surface of the water rippled.

And then it burst into flame.

A burst of bright light flared upon it as though lightning tore a midnight sky asunder. Images began to flower in rapid flashes—too rapid to trace, but branding themselves on Elric's mind like dreams on the cusp of waking.

He saw a youth in armor, not much older than he was himself, with storm-gray eyes that were a mirror image of his own. The youth danced fire and steel, slicing at black forms that screamed without a mouth. The armor smoldered, the battlefield blackened with smoke.

A flash of another moment: a tower disintegrating into swirling of fog, its top crumbling like a castle built on sand beneath the sea, and a thousand soundless voices whispering at a distance.

And then—a flame sigil spread out in the air, each petal a deep shade of dawn fire. Monsters with spiked hide and twisting horns trembled before it, their eyes bulging in some forgotten horror.

And finally—

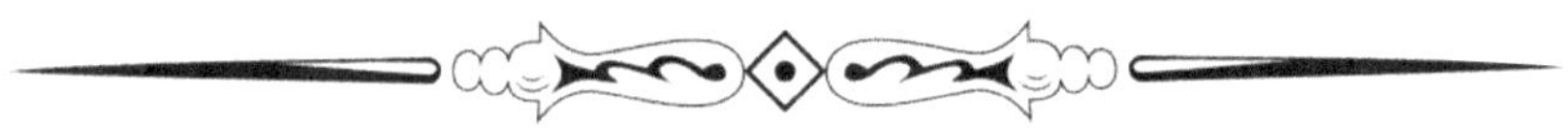

Elric, standing at the precipice alone. Wind howled at his mantle, and his eyes blazed—not with consideration, but inwardly. The same runes that had contorted under his feet now capered in his irises, pulsing with unguessable power.

He was not trembling.

But something in the forest was.

The pool darkened. The lights above it stopped moving. The silence came back-but now, it was deep. As if the grove itself had seen what he'd seen… and no longer knew what to make of him.

Nib looked up at him, eyes serious for the first time. "Well?"

"I saw. things," Elric said. "My dad. A tower. Magic everywhere. And me. But. not me."

"Looks like the forest thinks you have a part to play," Nib said. "A spark's been lit. Whether you burn or shine—that's up to you."

Elric leaned back, heart pounding.

His father was alive. Somewhere out there—in trouble, maybe, or fighting in the people's interest.

And now, somehow, he was a part of it.

He looked at Nib. "I need to find him."

Nib's whiskers trembled. "I figured you would."

He flew over to a bush and pulled out a bag nearly as big as he was. "Then we should get you a wand, a snack, and maybe a less burn-susceptible shirt."

Elric grinned, nerves buzzing. "You're coming with me?"

Nib snorted. "You'd get eaten before lunch without me."

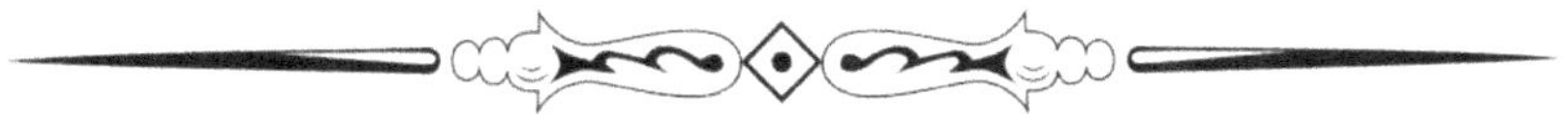

Together, they turned from the Glimmer well—and the forest closed behind them, sealing the memory like a secret, bearing within it something profound and persuasive.

But not before the runes lit up once more beneath Elric's feet.

Chapter Three

Wands, Warnings, and Wandering Mushrooms

Morning crept over the forest like a sleepy yawn over the forest horizon—soft gold seeping through leaves like a candle wax.

Elric awoke with a pinecone jammed into his spine and a disgruntled creature sprawled across his face.

"I warned you about moss pillows," Nib growled, pulling a twig from his ear and adjusting his acorn helmet. "They hold grudges, and they never forget."

Elric cracked one eye open. "I believe the moss tried to eat my boot overnight."

Nib didn't look impressed. "Could be worse. Last week, one tried to marry a shoe, at least it didn't try to marry it. That's happened before—messy annulment."

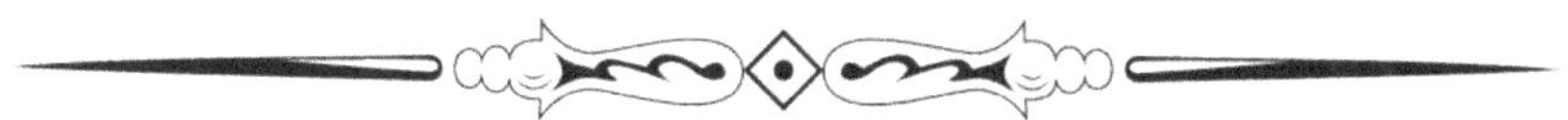

He rose, brushed bark crumbs from his cloak, and hoisted his satchel over his shoulder. "Sparkle fingers, up you get, let's get moving. Wand hunting lies ahead."

"Don't you mean wand seeking?"

Nib showed a flash of very pointy teeth. "Oh no. Hunting. These things travel."

Elric followed him along a narrow path rimmed with fluorescent mushrooms. They were for decoration, he supposed… until one growled, "Excuse you," when he nearly stepped on it.

"Wandering puffs rooms," Nib said as a pair of them huffed up in indignation and stomped off on tiny root legs. "Unreasonably proud. Petty. But excellent tea ingredients—if you survive the harvest.".

"Good to know," Elric said, going a large circle around the mushrooms. "Anything else I shouldn't touch?"

"Everything."

They passed through a veil of weeping vines—its tendrils soft as silk and fragrant with vanilla and ancient rain, the kind that holds the scent of memory and dust—they came into a clearing unlike any Elric had ever laid eyes on.

The air shifted. It didn't move—it was motionless, as if the world itself had drawn a deep, respectful breath.

Silence descended, not just as the absence of sound but as a presence, wide and watchful. It adhered to the gnarled trunks and hung between the pillars of gold light that permeated the canopy. It was the kind of silence that belonged to old things—things with roots older than stone and names no one had spoken in centuries.

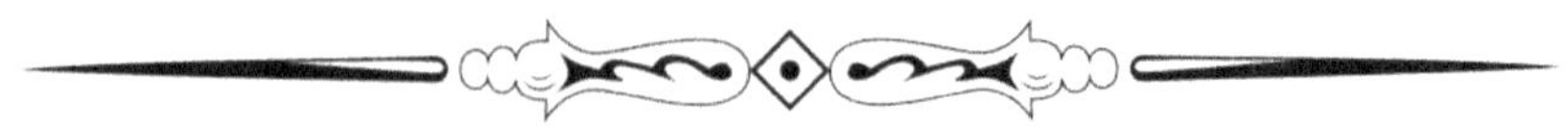

Elric paused. Even the wings of Nib fell silent, their usual nervous humming muted. The forest did not seem alive.

It was.

Every leaf listened. Every fern bowed in greeting or in warning. The moss beneath his feet was warm, as if the earth had been waiting for his tread.

He did not dare speak. Not because he was afraid—but because he respected it. This place did not need words. It needed remembering.

And Elric was aware, though no one told him, that the forest awaited him.

The trees stood ghostly tall and pale, with bark shining like pearls. Dangling among their boughs hung scores of wands, each floating as if without mass, revolving slowly on their axes. Some glittered gold, some softly glowed in strange hues—purple, green, sapphire blue.

"The Wand grove," Nib whispered, removing his hat in wonder.

Elric stepped ahead, and the atmosphere changed. It knew him.

Goosebumps prickled across his arms. His fingers twitched. Every wand seemed to tremble in anticipation, yet no one moved toward him.

He walked slowly, heart hammering. One wand—slender and elegant with a silver spiral—drifted closer, but as he reached out, it zipped away like a shy bird.

"You're trying too hard," Nib called gently. "Let them come to you."

Elric took a deep breath. He shut his eyes and stopped thinking about the competition. He wanted to get rid of the worry whether he was worthy enough to be chosen or not. If the runes had been a mistake, if his father would even recognize the boy he'd turned into.

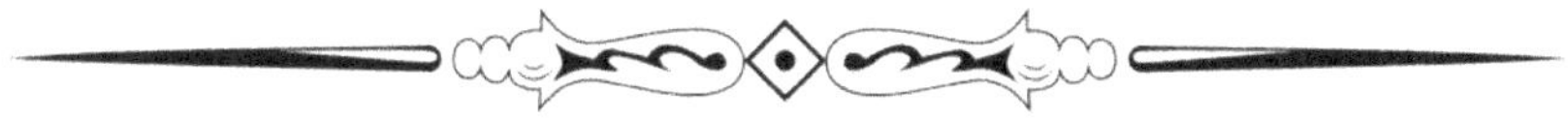

He just… let it all go.

And in that silence, he felt it.

A pull.

He opened his eyes and looked at it, tucked away under the rotting roots of a dead tree, half-buried in moss.

Bent, black, almost flat. A gnarled limb of dark reddish wood, wrapped in silver wire and etched with faint runes he couldn't read. It wasn't burning. It wasn't floating.

But it was waiting.

Elric stretched out—and as soon as his hand enclosed the wand, a light seemed to awaken in his chest, wild and golden, like fire flowing through his blood. It was not flames that blazed, but something ancient—a recollection of flame, of intent, of something within him stirring.

The runes on the staff came alive, their borders shimmering with light that appeared to be living. With them, the symbols etched on his arms also blazed in response, glowing together as if they had been waiting for this to happen.

For a heartbeat—the length of one—it lengthened almost too much, as if the wand was scanning him, taking account of him, weighing out every sin in his heart. And then it settled, nestling in him as if it were home.

The forest sighed.

And Elric knew—that was no ordinary wand.

It had chosen him.

And then, silence again.

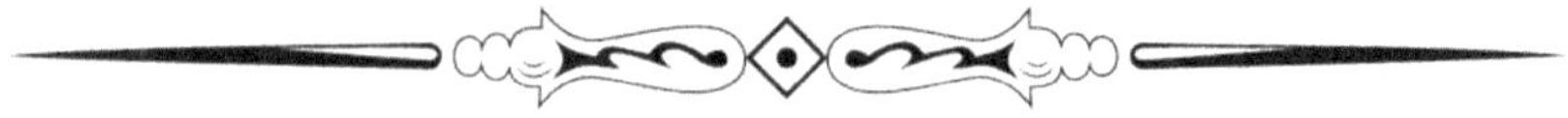

Elric rose, wand tight in his fist, and for the first time in his life, he felt seen.

Nib was still wide-eyed. "Well. That's. unexpected."

"Why?"

"That wand's been around for centuries. Nobody's ever so much as gotten it to blink."

Elric gazed at it. "What does that mean?"

Nib fluttered in close, his face creased. "It means the forest didn't just welcome you—it remembered you."

Before Elric could even ask what that meant, the sky ripped like glass about to shatter.

A deep, throaty howl echoed through the Wand grove—a sound so low it rattled Elric's ribs. Birds burst from the trees in a panicked flurry. Even the puffs rooms screamed (very high-pitched) and fled.

Nib's fur bristled. "Oh, brambleberry jam on burnt toast."

"What is it?"

"Hunter. From the East Plateau."

A deep, rasping howl traversed the Wand grove—a sound so primal and low it seemed to bubble up from beneath the very foundations of the earth itself. It vibrated Elric's ribs, shuddering in his bones like a warning bell clashing in his very blood. Birds took flight overhead across the trees, their wings beating the air in a chaotic, desperate scramble.

Even the puffs rooms—normally impassive to storms, swords, or bellowing—pumped out a chorus of high-pitched squeaks and scurried away like popcorn over flames.

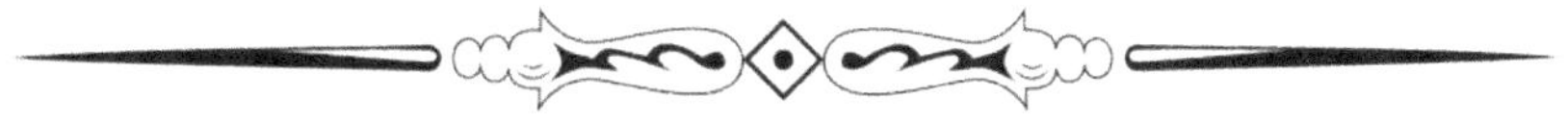

Nib's fur stood on end, every hair quivering like a struck dandelion. He sniffed, sneezed twice, and halted.

"Ah," he gasped, restricted voice, "brambleberry jam on black toast."

Elric grasped his wand. "What is it?"

Nib didn't twitch an eyelash. "Hunter. From the East Plateau."

The Wand grove withered into a dry silence.

Elric stooped low beside a fern that radiated dew, his breathing measured, his heartbeat ticking loud enough to number. The forest itself shook—leaves rolling up, birdsong abandoned, even the dust motes of sunlight above the roots ceased.

Nib hovered beside him, wings beating with anxious hum. "Don't move. Don't breathe too hard. Plateau hunters don't just pursue. They stalk. They listen. They sense."

A piercing gust roughened the leaves above. Something creaked. Not wind—weight. Heavy. Measured.

Elric's eyes moved downwards. On the moss beside the gnarled trunk of a birch was a print not booted. Not human. A three-fingered imprint, deep, charred around the edges as if the earth had been seared. The moss nearby had died to black.

"Elric..." Nib breathed, the eyes narrowing. "That's not a hunter. That's a Bound One. They use cursed magic to bind beasts and men to their will."

More tracks appeared—splayed and irregular, like the beast was dragging something heavy behind it. Claw marks had stripped the bark from nearby trees in angry slashes. Dark smear glistened on a rock—not blood, not sap. It smelled of ash and ozone.

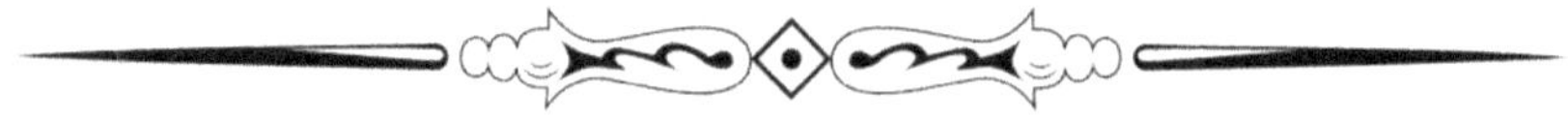

"Whatever it is," Elric breathed, "it's close."

He took a step forward to the next tree, and stopped.

The trunk was etched with symbols—those same, writhing runes carved deep and softly glowing. Those same runes which had burned under his feet.

"They're hunting you," Nib growled low. "But not with claws and curses. With your own kind of magic."

Elric stepped back, but the rune glowed hotter.

And from a distance in front, behind a veil of thorn-horned fog, a figure moved.

He pointed at Elric.

"The forest has spoken out," he growled. "And it has chosen… wrong."

Elric raised his wand instinctively, although he had no idea what to do with it. "I—I don't want to fight you!"

The hunter advanced. "Then die quickly."

The hunter attacked in a flash.

The trees shuddered.

The shadow stepped closer, and now Elric had a good view of it: part man, part monstrosity. Its skin was striped with binding runes like scars, its eyes blank but burning pale blue, as if filled from within. In one hand it dragged a barbed spear still dripping dark sap.

The air turned colder.

Elric lifted his wand.

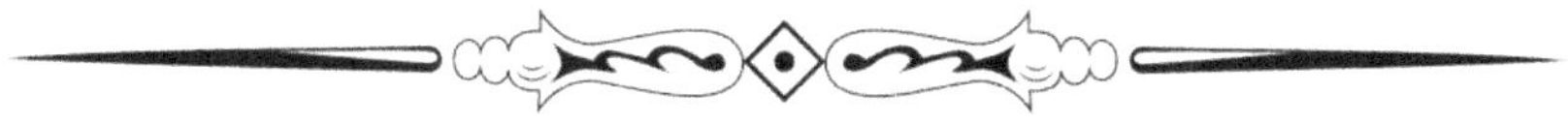

And something happened.

Light exploded from its tip—not flame, not lightning, but a blast of pure, radiant energy. A radiant shockwave sent the hunter stumbling backwards, tearing through two trees and culminating in a heap of shrieking puffs rooms. They squealed in high, panicked tones and scattered in all directions, vanishing in puffs of spores.

"Whoa," Nib breathed, wings fluttering. "Okay. That wasn't in the forest guide."

But the hunter wasn't finished.

It stood with a grind of scraping stone. Half of its mask was split open, revealing a snarl of teeth too long, too sharp. It bellowed—and the runes on its chest blazed like coals in a furnace.

Its spear sprang from its hand of its own accord. It arced towards Elric.

He dodged just in time—but the spear struck the trunk behind him with a muted THUNK, splitting it with a boom like thunder.

"Elric! Focus!" Nib shouted, weaving upwards in a zigzag pattern. "The runes—you bear them too! Let them direct—"

The hunter attacked.

Elric whirled around, raising the wand again. This time, he made no effort to force the magic.

He let it come.

The runes on his arms erupted into life, swirling up into his shoulders like fireflies. The wand pulsed. And from its core, a lash of golden vines snapped outwards—real vines, stitched with light—entwining the hunter's legs in mid-charge.

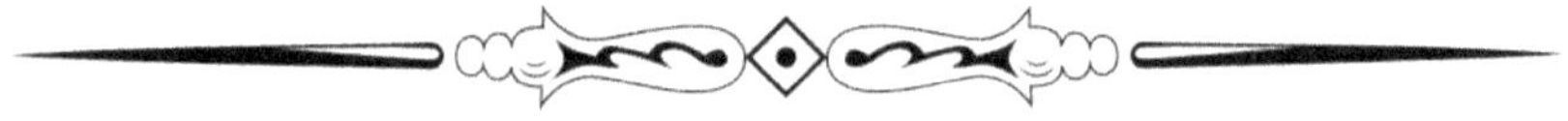

It went down with a snarl, crashing into the earth.

Elric dashed forwards, his breath rasping in his throat. "This has to stop."

The hunter growled, struggling, then shrieked—a horrid, vacant sound that made even the light falter.

Then… from the forest itself there was an answer.

The trees groaned. Roots shifted. A whispering choir echoed, not in Elric's ears, but in his bones.

The forest had wakened.

Vines—not of light, but of wood and moss—burst from the ground, from tree trunks, from hidden crevices. They grasped the hunter, encasing him, pulsing with a muffled hum.

The runes on the creature's chest fluttered, then… went out.

The forest was quiet again.

Elric dropped to his knees, the wand inert in his hand. His arms still glowed softly, pulsing with breath-like rhythm.

Nib floated beside him, quiet.

"You're changing," Nib said softly. "You're not just using magic, Elric. You're becoming part of it."

Elric blinked, staring at his wand, gasping. "Did I… do that?"

Nib nodded. "You certainly did.

As the vines finished wrapping up the first hunter, and the forest grew still, Elric exhaled a shuddery breath. Nib landed on his shoulder, saying, "Good shot for someone who doesn't know what they're doing."

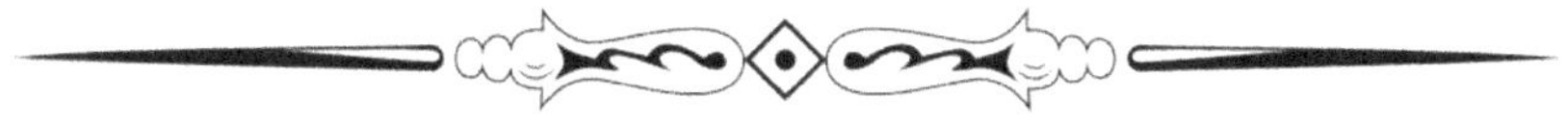

But then—

Snap.

A branch snapped behind them.

Elric spun around. Nib's wings snapped open.

From out of the mist between two bent trees stepped a second figure—slimmer, silent, in robes that shimmered like spider silk and ash. She wore no mask. Her face was white, painted with identical runes, eyes a pale violet that glowed in the dark. A curving blade of bone was tied at her back, and she bore no weapon—yet Elric felt a deeper danger from her than from the one still wrapped in roots.

She tilted her head. "Well done, boy. The forest likes you."

Elric's grip on the wand tightened. "Who are you?"

"I'm not here for conversation." She stepped forward, and as her foot touched the moss, the plants beneath withered. "I'm here for you."

The ground shuddered.

"Elric—she's not like the other one," Nib hissed, hiding behind his collar. "She's a whisper-binder."

Elric didn't know what that was, but it sounded bad. "Why are you pursuing me?"

"Because you touched the Wand grove," she said softly. "Because you broke the seal. Because your blood remembers what your mind has forgotten."

Elric's runes began to glow again—but floundered. Unbalanced. Weakened by the previous spell.

She saw.

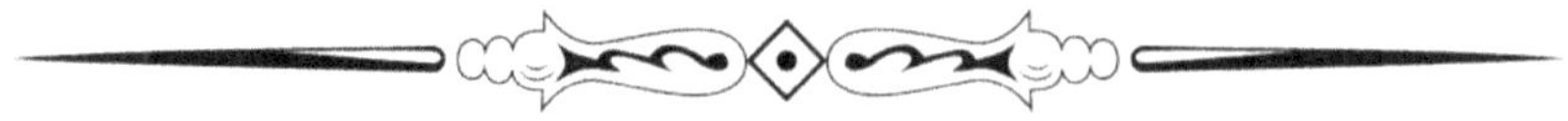

And smiled.

With a flash of speed, she was on him—too quickly. Elric hardly raised the wand, and nothing happened this time.

She gripped his wrist.

The runes flared—both of them.

Agony shot up his arm. Visions. Too quick, too vivid to cling to: fire-tower blazing, mask shattering, his father into darkness falling.

Then—light.

The first hunter, the one still trapped, screamed. The vines tightened. The ground cracked.

The woman flinched—hardly.

Elric ripped free, fell back, and stuck the wand in the earth.

A ring of light roots curled out like a shockwave, propelling her back. She flowed, sure-footed, and vanished between the trees with a whisper of air and scattering blossoms.

Silence fell again, dense and uncertain.

"Elric…" Nib said firmly, "We have to go. Now. If she is here, others will be too."

Elric nodded, pounding heart, wand still in his grasp.

Whatever it was. It had just begun.

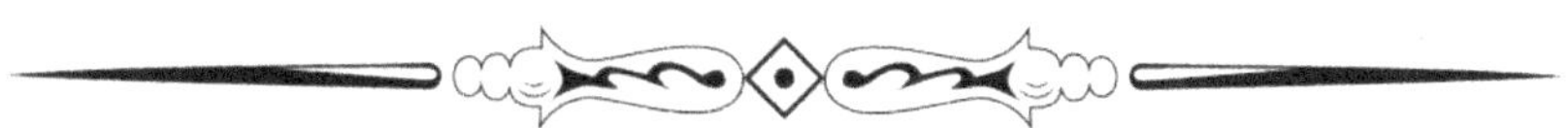

Chapter Four
Fire and Fog

The trees blurred past as Elric and Nib ran, dodging tangled roots and flailing branches like dancers in a nightmare ballet.

"Left!" Nib screeched.

Elric veered hard—just in time to miss a tree that dropped a bucket-load of sap with suspicious aim.

Behind them, the forest trembled with the furious roar of the Plateau hunters. Birds scattered. The trees hissed warnings in creaky groans. The very earth seemed to wince beneath their steps.

"They are fast!" Elric panted, clutching the wand tight.

"Fast, angry, and hunting us through a cursed forest. This is *not* the scenic route I had in mind!" Nib yelled, vaulting over a glowing mushroom that exploded into glittery mist.

A low whistling sound filled the air. Elric turned his head.

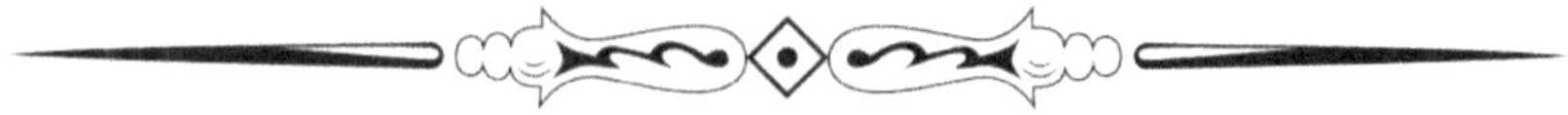

An arrow whistled past—then another. One grazed his sleeve. The third stuck in a tree ahead and *exploded* into sparks.

"THEY HAVE BOOM-BOWS?" Elric shrieked.

"New development! I hate new developments!" Nib cried, zigzagging wildly.

They burst into a sudden clearing—but this one was different.

Thick, unnatural fog hung low over the ground. It swirled in slow spirals, coiling like snakes. The trees were stunted here, warped as if melted. The light had a coppery tint, like the sun was bleeding.

"Where are we?" Elric asked, chest heaving.

Nib stopped, sniffed the air, and groaned. "Oh."

"Oh *no,* what?"

"This is *Cinder hollow.* The burned part of the forest. It never fully died, but it never healed either."

"Is it dangerous?"

Nib didn't answer at once. His wings drooped. Even his otherwise sunny eyes dimmed.

"It's worse than dangerous," he finally snarled. "It remembers."

Elric looked around at the gnarled trees, the burned bark curled like wrinkled parchment. Shadows capered in the mist, but there was no wind. The copper light threw everything into battered hues.

"Remember what?" he asked.

Nib swallowed. "The fire. The wars. The magic that tore it apart. Pain like this doesn't go away, it simmers. Sometimes the forest weeps here. Sometimes it bites."

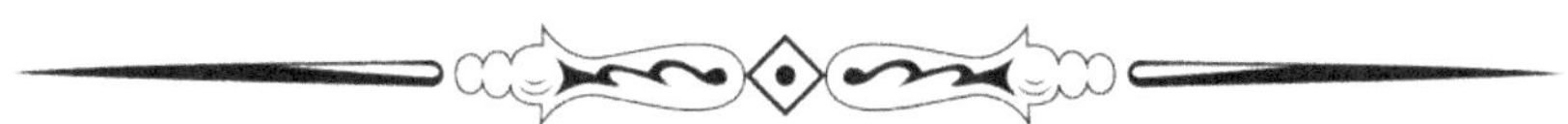

A faint hiss echoed through the mist. The spirals pulled in even tighter, twisting with intent now.

Elric raised his wand.

Nothing moved. Not yet.

And something stirred under the ground—like a network of roots, twisting. The earth steamed. A dead tree beside it groaned and split down the middle. Something emerged from of it—skeletal, wood-like, and steaming, as if still smoldering from years past.

A Burn-walker.

Nib shrieked and hid behind Elric's head. "Don't let it touch you!"

Elric retreated a step, wand glowing faintly. "Why?"

"Because it is made of memory. And it wants yours."

The Burn walker lurched, spasming limbs and rattling moan, smoke curling from its sockets.

Elric didn't waste time. He thrust his wand out, flaring the runes—not just with power this time, but will. He pictured light. Life. Cool forest air and leaves rustling.

A pulse of silver emanated from the wand, catching the Burn walker mid-charge.

It stopped. Shuddered. The rolling smoke around it turned white—and then, in a parched, empty gasp, burst asunder like dried bark and rained down to ash.

The fog quieted once more. More hisses. Wood snapping far away.

"That was just one," Nib hushed. "We should go. Before the others wake."

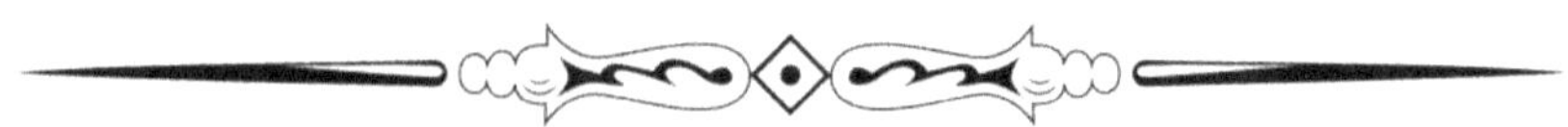

"But where?" Elric whirled around, dizzy, lost in the swirling fog.

And then, in the mist—a whisper.

"Elric…"

He froze. The voice was gentle, one he recognized.

"Elric…"

His father's voice. He turned around.

"No!" Nib yelled. "Don't listen. It's the Hollow calling—it uses the ones you miss."

But Elric had already walked towards him.

Elric paused, mist fogging in copper light. The fog coiled round him, creeping up his boots.

And then he heard it—A voice, silken and crackly as aged paper.

"Elric…"

His head snapped round towards the sound.

A figure stepped out of the mist—tall, shadow-shrouded, but discernible. The hunch of the shoulders. The way it walked. The voice again, low and pleading:

"It's me. Don't be afraid, son."

Nib locked his ankle. "Elric. Don't."

"Not—I just have to be sure." Elric's voice cracked. "It sounded like—like him."

The figure coalesced into sight—half-formed, as smoke on the edge of a dream. It was his father's armor. His father's eyes. But when it grinned… it was wrong. Too many teeth. And no warmth in the eyes.

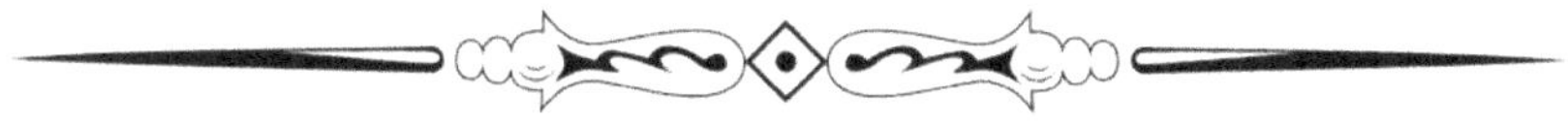

Elric took one shaking step forward, then stopped. His hand contracted around his wand.

What did you tell me the last time we spoke before the war?" Elric demanded.

The thing twitched.

"We. We exchanged our farewells."

"No," Elric panted. "You instructed me to protect Mother. You'd be back. You promised."

The creature spat.

The trickery dissipated like smoke blown upon by wind—revealing something bony and pale and multi-armed, huddled where the voice had been. A Hollow Mimic.

It screamed and struck out. Elric thrust his wand forward, light flashing.

"You're not him!

A blinding flash of light burst from the tip—enough to push it back into the fog.

He wasted no time. Elric spun and fled.

And behind them, the fog howled.

Elric stood alone in the clearing, panting.

Then—*thud.*

A massive shape dropped from the tree above.

The hunter landed with unnatural grace, eyes glowing like twin coals.

Elric's heart dropped.

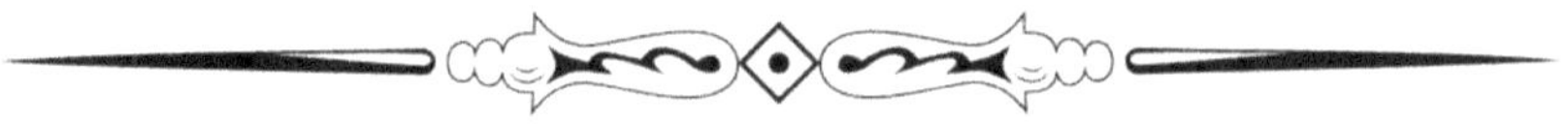

"Found you," the hunter growled.

"I wasn't hiding," Elric said.

The wand shimmered in his hand. The hunter charged.

He lifted the wand, felt the runes along his arm burning with power—and shouted a word he didn't know he knew.

A wall of flame roared from the earth, encircling them both.

The hunter halted, eyes narrowing. "Forbidden magic…"

The fire hissed and danced, forming shapes—dragons, symbols, swords.

"I don't want to fight," Elric said, steadily.

"Then surrender."

"I can't. I have to find my father."

The hunter hesitated. Then—for the first time—she looked… uncertain.

"You wear his face," the hunter said. "You carry his fire."

"What?"

The hunter stepped back into the mist—and vanished.

The fire died down.

Nib stumbled into view, coughing. "Elric? You, okay?"

Elric nodded slowly. "I think so."

"What did you *do*?"

"I don't know. But I think the wand does."

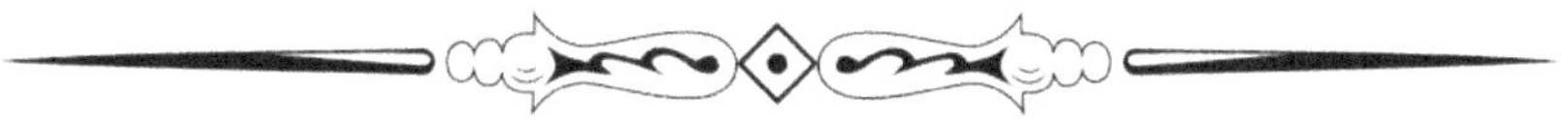

He looked down at the wooden wand, his hand—no longer just a tool.

It was a key. A torch. A path.

"I think we just started something big," Elric said.

Nib looked around at the fog curling away, and the scorched ground where the hunter had stood.

"Yeah," he said. "And we'll need marshmallows."

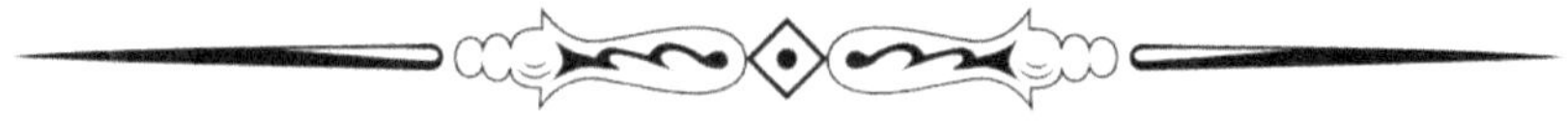

Chapter Five
The Map That Shouldn't Exist

That night, Elric slept.

It was no repose, but a plunge into a maelstrom of fire and shadow.

Trees charred by fire creaked and groaned like grieving giants, their limbs reaching for him with burning, crimson fingers. Mist crept through the air, not cold, but sighing—whispering in a language he almost knew. Shapes danced behind it, too swift to distinguish but too familiar to be ignored.

And then—A face.

Nothing strange or inhumane. But rather something familiar.

A tall, brawny man. Burning armor. An outstretched palm. Eyes that looked exactly like Elric's. Yet no matter how desperately he stretched to reach the image, it ran away from him like water between his fingers.

He woke up before dawn, gasping, the memory itself already lost—except for one thing:

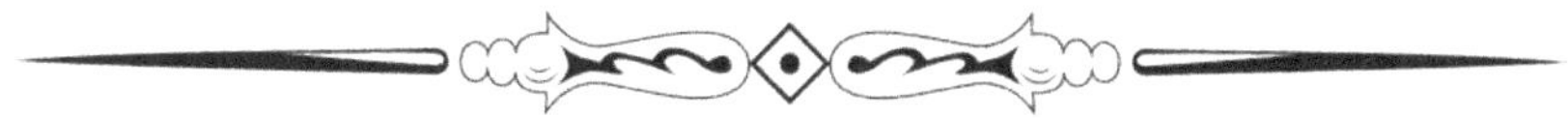

The face in the mist had called him by name.

"Elric…"

Elric sat up and pulled the wand from his belt. Its grain shimmered faintly in the dawn light. Strange runes had appeared overnight along the grip—some glowed dimly, others pulsed like heartbeat rhythms.

He didn't remember casting them.

"I'm either very gifted," he muttered, "Or slightly cursed."

"Little of column A, lots of column B," came Nib's muffled voice from under his cloak.

Elric turned. "You're awake?"

"Only because my dreams were invaded by sassy mushrooms." Nib sat up, rubbed his eyes, then yawned. "One of them had a monocle and tried to teach me accounting."

"Useful."

"Terrifying."

They both laughed softly—but the mood quickly faded. The events of the night before pressed down on them like a heavy mist.

"We have to keep moving," Elric said. "I don't know where the hunter got off to, but I'll wager he was not done."

"True enough," Nib said, brushing leaves from his shoulder.

Elric looked at the wand.

It beckoned.

Not straight, not in a beam or light—but it tugged at something inside him. An instinct, a pull just behind his ribs.

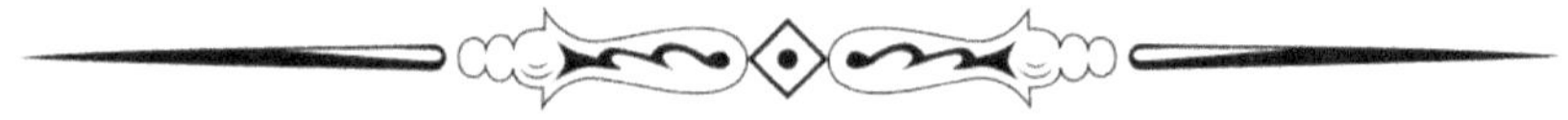

Nodding, he pointed the way.

"Go on," he said, walking away. "This way."

They moved through the morning forest, lighter now but still wary. Birds sang warily, and branches quivered overhead even when there was no wind.

Hours went by.

They passed over a brook where the stream ran uphill, and skirted a sleeping stone golem who grumbled in sleep of "lost mountains."

At last, the trees thinned out—and they stepped into a glade unlike any other.

A tree stood at its center. Not—a tree. A tree sculpture, crafted from smooth roots and glass wrapped in vines.

Teeny lights swirled around it like stars.

"'The Wand grove," Nib whispered, his voice instantly hushed in awe.

"You recognize it?"

"I am aware of it. This spot is old—older than the oldest map. Every wand constructed using soul wood is from this grove. And it is said… occasionally, it provides something in return."

Elric stepped nearer. The air around here was chilly, clean, and magical.

The tree pulsed with life.

He waved out his wand—and the tree responded.

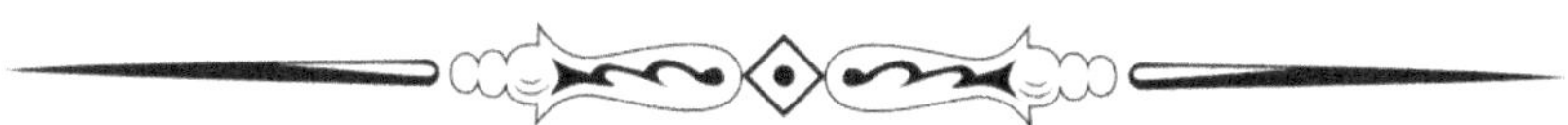

Its vines wrapped tenderly around him, caressing wood, and yanking away suddenly, as from a shock. One of the glass leaves splintered—then fell.

Elric grabbed it.

And when he did—the grove changed.

The lights spun faster, coming together into patterns of stars.

Signs cut in the grass—maps of the old cartographers and forgotten roads.

And in Elric's palm, the leaf of magic glowed—and unfolded into something impossible.

A map.

But not one drawn on parchment.

It floated out of his hand, lines of enchantment incising canyons, valleys, tunnels, and fortresses. A glittering marker throbbed with fiery light at the border—his father's location.

Elric stepped back; air caught in his throat.

Nib gazed. "That's… That's not merely an isthmus map. That's the Threads. A map of what was, what is, and what might be."

"Why is it showing me this?"

"Because it chose you," a voice behind them replied.

They turned—only to find an old woman in billowy robes, bark-like skin, moss-and-moonlight hair.

"You are the keeper of the Wand grove's secret," she said, eyes glinting. "And now… you must bear its weight."

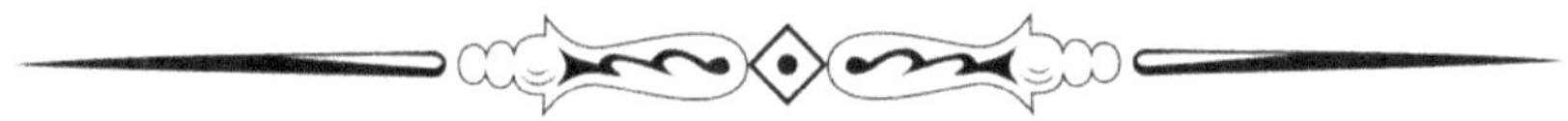

Elric scowled. "Who are you?"

"I am the Guardian of the Grove. It's the last speaker. And I know what you are seeking: your father, the truth of the war, and your place in both."

Elric grasped the glowing map tightly. "Then, help me."

She shook her head and, gradually, the fire's dance was mirrored in her eyes.

"I will," she breathed, muttered. "But you must understand—this isn't about one man… or even one family."

She looked out over the darkening horizon, where forest pressed up against the far peaks.

"This war—the one you see on the surface—was ignited by mortals. Greed. Fear. Power. But something is getting older. Something written in flame and forbidden runes. Seethes beneath it all."

Her gaze returned to Elric, resolute now.

"If we're not cautious, we won't lose the war. We'll wake what lies beneath it."

Elric met her gaze. "Then I'll finish it."

Even Nib flinched at that.

The Guardian smiled very lightly, as if to see a long-faded star come alive again.

"Very well," she said. "Then you must go east—beyond the Shatter spires. To a location that has no right to exist."

Elric looked down at the floating map.

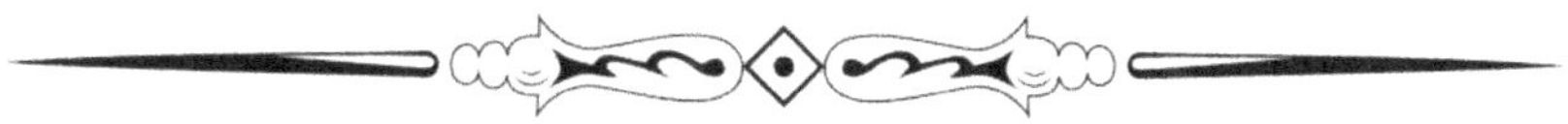

The red flashing beat moved—towards the mountains on the edge of the mapped world.

And towards the road to his father.

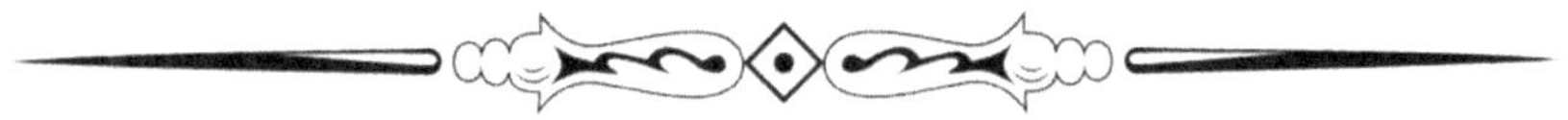

Chapter Six
The Shatter spires

The higher they climbed, the thinner the air grew.

The quiet mosses and rustling trees of the forest were lost—now the ground was broken, serrated with shale, and the wind howled like a living creature. Ahead of them loomed the Shatter spires, a continuous line of twisted mountains, their crests pointing towards the sky like shattered teeth.

Elric wrapped his cloak tighter. The map—no more than a splinter of light now, folded deep within a hidden pouch—quivered with every step, drawing him ever eastward.

Nib was uncharacteristically silent.

"You all, right?" Elric asked, glancing back.

Nib looked up from atop a rock he'd been examining. "I'm okay. Just, uneasy. Places like this? Mountains that don't follow the laws of nature, stones that sing when no one is listening. I don't trust it."

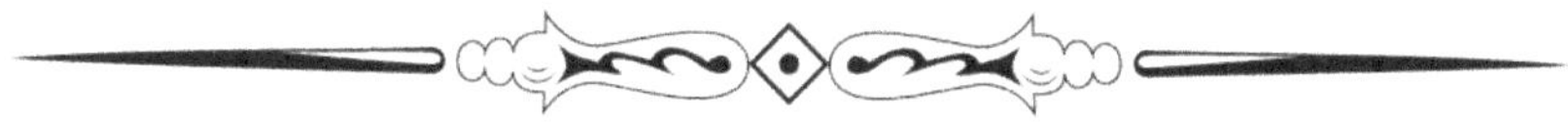

Elric nodded. He understood too well. The path proceeded between two shattered rocks, worn into strange, spiral furrows—as if some immense something had passed through again and again, centuries ago.

Between them, as they passed through, a gentle sound met their ears. No wind. Not stone.

Singing.

Low and slurred, it was echoed softly over the cliffs. Not in words Elric knew, but full of sorrow, rising and dipping as an old forgotten nursery rhyme. The sound twisted his gut.

Nib stopped halfway up a step. "That's spire-song," he whispered. "Rock ghosts. Or something worse."

Elric whirled around. "You mean, worse than rock ghosts?"

Nib nodded solemnly. "The sort that reminds you when you leave.".

They went on, more subdued now. Shadows capered at the edge of Elric's vision—stone faces, crack eyes, claw-talented dust that shifted—but whenever he looked straight at them, they disappeared.

Another mile passed. The path widened, revealing a narrow bridge of broken slate spanning a deep mist-choked ravine.

Along the span, embedded in the rock as an unwelded wound, was a downed tower of black glass. The map in Elric's pouch pulsed to the rhythm of life.

"That's it," he said. "The next marker."

Nib frowned. "That's no tower. That's a shard spire. Sheared off during the first War of Flame. They claim it was a spire of a temple that tried to hold back the ancient magic.".

As if in agreement, the earth beneath them groaned.

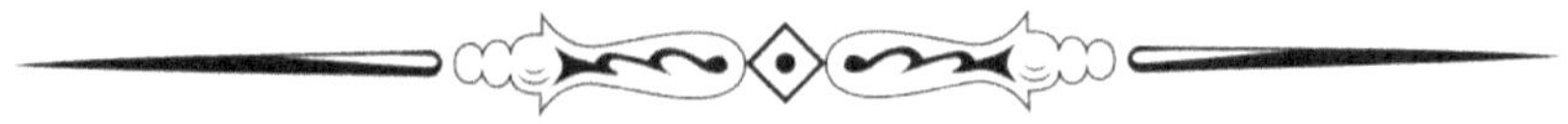

Elric caught his breath. "Come on. Let's cross before whatever its holding down decided to wake."

"The Guardian told us to go through them."

"She also told us we'd need more than bravery."

As if summoned by her words, the wind changed.

It carried with it a low, rasping echo—something enormous scraping on gravel. And then the laughter.

Not human.

Not quite alive either.

Elric slowed. "What was that?"

Nib's ears pricked. "Trouble. Big, echo-y, probably-too-many-teeth trouble."

They pushed on now, climbing up a twisted goat trail, where rocks glowed blue with an odd sheen. Clouds curled through the valleys below them like sleeping dragons. After nearly an hour, they reached a thin ledge.

And there, reclining on a natural rock pedestal like a throne, was a being.

It was human-form—but impossibly tall, draped in tattered pennants of ash-gray silk. Its face was carved stone, cracked and aglow with light from within. Ember eyes. Thunder voice.

"You carry the Wand grove's spark," it bellowed.

Elric tried to speak, but the words caught in his throat.

The monster stood. Its legs splintered the ground. "Many have tried to cross the Spires. Most die. Some are eaten. A few. are turned."

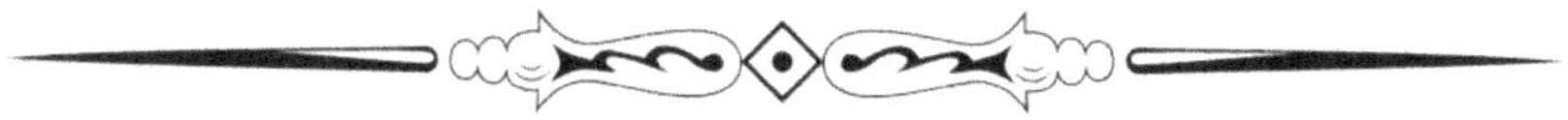

"Turned into what?" Nib breathed.

"Echoes. Shadows of who they used to be. Stone travelers and sorrow." The Sentinal said.

Elric moved forward a step. "We have to go through. My father's past this boundary. He's a soldier—missing in action."

The monster leaned forward, tipping its head.

"The war is merely a surface. A gossamer film above what lies below."

"You know something?"

"I know that which lies in darkness beneath these summits. I am the Sentinel. Keeper of Wounds. And I watch the way."

He leaned over them, knees bent and knees threatening, his eyes aflame like burning stars.

"But to walk upon it, you have to surrender something."

Elric's pulse slammed in his ears. "What?"

"A memory. A truth. Or a fear."

Nib raised an eyebrow. "That's. rather inconvenient."

Elric remained still. "Why?"

"Because the mountains are alive. They remember what you give them—and use it against you." the Sentinel said.

The silence stretched out a very long time.

Then Elric took a step forward.

He recalled the ballad his mother sang, hummed low and deliberate on stormy nights lightning split the heavens and thunder boomed like a

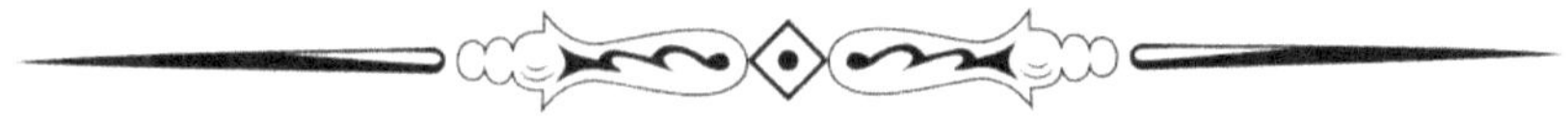

drum in battle on the roof. Her voice had enveloped him like wool, worn and frayed with love. He recalled the gentle pull of her fingers through his hair, the scent of woodsmoke and lavender clinging to her robe. The way she'd talked of tales—of dragons rolled about beneath the moon, breathing slow, dreaming in gold sleep, waiting for the world to need them again.

The memory swelled in his chest—pulsing and aching.

He closed his eyes—and let go.

It hurt. Not the ache a wound would seep, but the manner in which absence could echo through your bones. The moment slipped past him like mist between fingers, leaving the heat, but not the details.

The Sentinel, as ancient and still as a statue carved from the heart of the mountain, drew a slow, whistling breath in through its hollow chest.

"A gentle one," it answered, voice sounding like gravel filled with thunder. "A vision in light. You can pass… but warned—are that what you relinquish can torment you."

Its melted silver eyes flashed once—then dimmed.

And before them the way was open.

Behind him, the mountain curved. Rocks groaned and shifted out of the way, revealing a narrow road of glowing stones—deeper into the Shatterspires' heart.

Elric encountered Nib. "Are you listening?"

"Sure thing," the small monster snarled. "But if a rock tries to whisper my name, I'm kicking it off a cliff."

And so they entered the mountain—where memories stirred, and darkness waited.

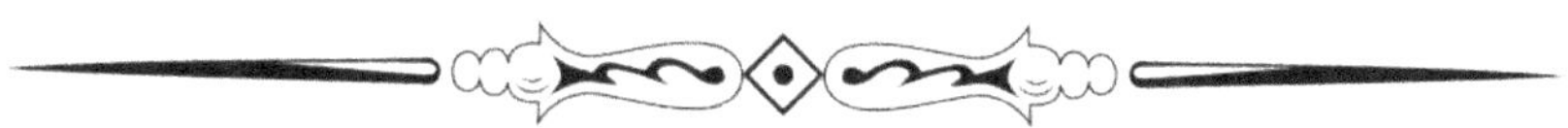

Chapter Seven

The Plateau's Shadow

The terrain beyond the Shatter spires changed, it was not what Elric expected.

No towering mountains were in sight. No glittering trails bending elegantly to the horizon. A grayish-green bog stretched instead, long and jagged and scarred-looking—still, stagnant, and infinite.

The ground pulled at Elric's boots with each step, invoking the smell of rotting vegetation and something far deeper—metallic and pungent, like rust-hued blood. Stagnant pools of water reflected a sallow sky, glinting not with light but with the dull shine of decay. The trees here were not trees, at least not anymore. They were distorted, grotesque things—trunks bent like splintered limbs, bark twisted into convulsive faces, as though they had crawled from the ground in pain.

Insects hung in slow spirals, hovering on near-invisible wings that clicked an chimed instead of humming - glasslike, rhythmic, unnerving. It sounded like time ticking in the heart of the bog, with a light that was

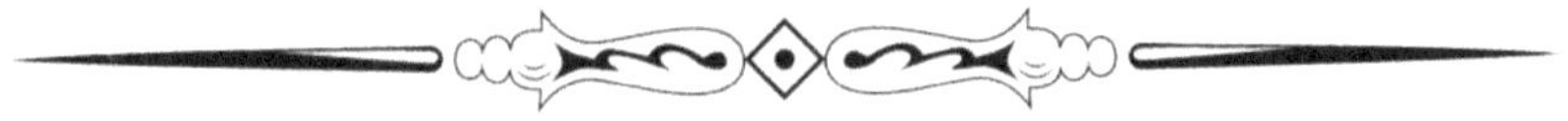

nearly liquid. They did not hum. They chimed, their wings clicking and clinking in an unsettling rhythm as though the bog itself was ticking… waiting.

Nib settled on Elric's shoulder, shuddering. "Ugh. Even the air tastes disgusting."

Elric swallowed hard. It did—thick and heavy, salt-tasting and sulfur-scented. He took another step forward, and the mud complained in protest under his foot, exhaling a thin steam.

"This place," he breathed, squinting at the horizon, "remembers everything that died here."

"I miss solid ground," complained Nib, pulling his feet out of yet another patch of tugging mud. "And air that isn't reeking of mildew and betrayal."

Elric remained silent. His eyes were already scanning the horizon, where the mist of the Plateau lingered—dark and saw-toothed in the distance, like a sleeping monster under a thundercloud.

They continued on.

The marsh gave way, at last, to rolling meadows filled with soft, golden grass and floating specks of light. It should have been beautiful.

But the flowers whispered.

Whenever he turned his head, Elric swore he heard whispery voices, half-laughing, half-crying. The petals followed him when he walked, always inclining toward his shadow.

"This whole place is wrong," he said finally.

Nib nodded. "Cursed marshes. Blessed meadows. It's as if the earth's been wounded—and it's dreaming wide awake."

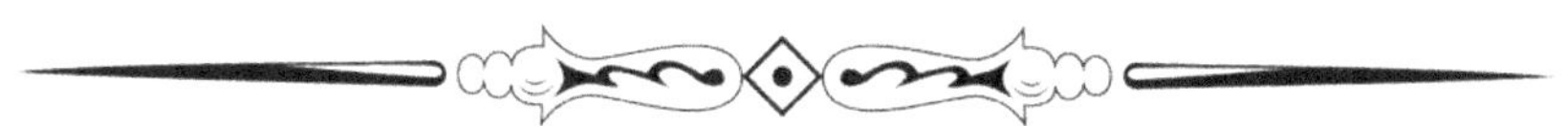

That's when they came into town.

Or what remained of town, anyway. Broken-down houses fell against each other like a chain of stumblebums, their walls weary with age and wear. Window casings yawned open like empty sockets. Roofs had fallen in under flames or age, and soot stained every stone—smudges of a memory no rain had erased. Vines spread through the ruins, threading like outstretched fingers, as if the earth itself were trying to reclaim what war had ravaged.

Elric stepped around an iron pot, half-buried under rubble, and halted when the wind changed. The quiet here wasn't quiet of peace, this was a muted quiet, as if the world was holding its breath.

In the middle of the ruined square stood a statue.

Or what remained of one.

It had once been proud—an armed knight, sword raised to the heavens. But it now stood decapitated, its head missing, the sword chipped and resting more at an angle to the earth than to the heavens. Black smudges marred its surface, and the base was scorched as if by lightning or worse.

It was the symbol carved in the stone, however, which took Elric's breath.

A ring of four ugly gouges, hacked inward like claws—or something else.

Nib dangled at his shoulder, saying, "That's a war-brand."

"What does it mean?"

Nib's wings fluttered. "It means that this was not just destroyed. This was cursed. That sign—it's ancient Plateau magic. Forbidden, even to them." he whispered.

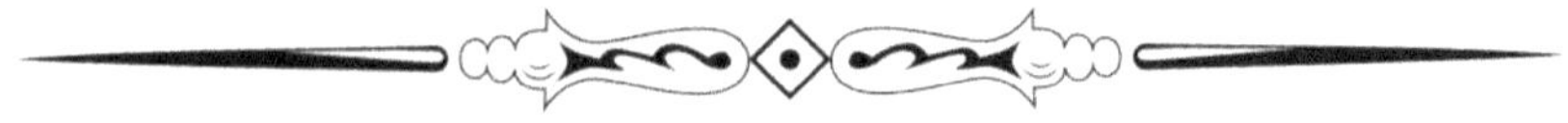

Elric took a step back. The wind curled around him, chill now, weaving through the ruined town like a half-finished memory.

"Let's not tarry," Nib growled.

Elric complied—but his eyes never left the target. There was something there that stirred in him, some memory not his own, or some warning too late spoken.

"The mark of the Plateau," a voice behind them said.

They turned hastily.

From the shadows of a ruined bakery, a figure emerged —slow, deliberate, and almost spectral. She moved like mist, her body blurring at the edges, as if the ruins breathed her into form, her presence muted but firm. Her gaunt face blended into the wreckage that surrounded her, as if she was part of it, or its part of her. For a moment, Elric wasn't certain she was real at all.

Her hair tumbled down her back in bone-white spirals, braided with the silver of ash and age. Her complexion was as pale as moonlight, and her eyes—pale green—sparkled like new leaves that had endured a frost. Clear-cut and sharp. Observing.

An elf.

Elric's fingers grew rigid, his other hand edging toward his wand.

Nib, however, had already edged several steps backward, half-hidden behind the remnants of an old cask. His wings vibrated once, nervous.

The girl had not reached for a weapon. She remained standing, waiting for them, with the quiet confidence of a predator—tensioned, amused, and fatigued. "Easy," she said, her voice husky and arid. "If I'd had you killed, I would have done it the third time you had all gotten yourself caught in the reeds."

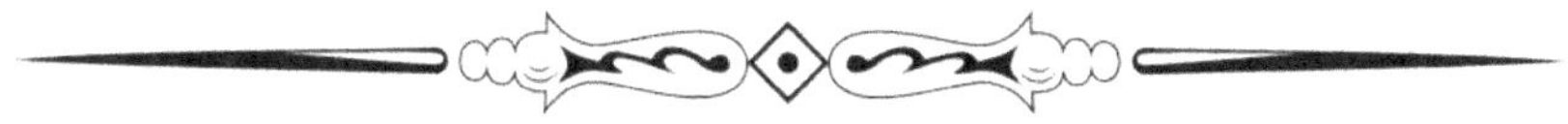

Elric blinked. "You were stalking us?"

She raised an eyebrow. "Hard not to. You weren't exactly elegant." She walked forward, her boots quiet on the broken stone, like a ghost walking through memory. "I just wanted to see if you arrived. Obviously, you did."

Elric hesitated, then bowed his head. "I'm Elric."

"Nib," a voice said from behind the barrel.

The elf turned that way, unmoved. "Call me Liora.".

Something about her name settled heavily in the air, like it carried more weight than just identity. She looked them both over again, her eyes pausing briefly on the pack Elric carried—on the faint glow still leaking from the hidden map.

"You're not just lost travelers," she said flatly.

"We're looking for someone," Elric replied, not offering more.

Liora's remained composed, her expression firm, but something behind her eyes tightened, a string drawn to its breaking point.

"Aren't we all," she said softly.

She turned, her voice barely above a whisper. "Come with me—if you want to survive tonight."

They bedded down that evening beneath the destroyed eaves of what had been a chapel—tilted stone pillars and a green-veined altar, nothing now. Above them, the sky gave no stars, only a feathery veil of clouds lit from below by far-off fires.

Elric kindled the flame with a puff of air from his wand, though it flickered oddly in this place—bluer than gold. It cast long shadows across the shattered tiles.

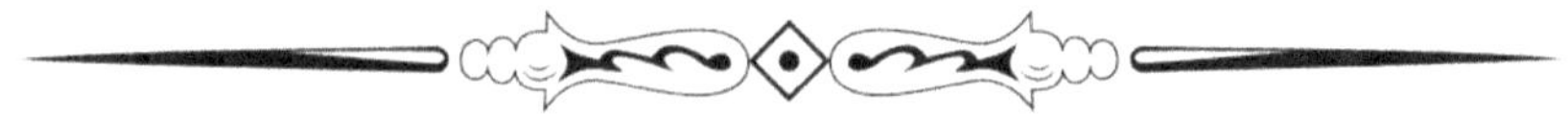

Nib curled up against the edge, already snoring into his acorn helmet.

Liora sat alone, against a crumbling pillar, legs tucked in tight, eyes half-shut but not sleeping. She was sharpening a fine blade, slow, ritualistic strokes ringing across the stillness.

Elric gazed at her. "So. you live out here? In the ruins?"

"I move," she said matter-of-factly. "No one lives in a place like this. They just wait."

He prodded the fire with a stick. Embers wafted up like fireflies. "Waiting for what?"

She was quiet for an extended period of time. Then: "An opportunity. For a weakness in the Plateau's defenses. Something to strike. An opening."

Elric stared at her. "You've fought them before."

"Yes."

He waited. When she failed to continue, he asked softly, "Did they take someone from you, too?"

Her hands slowed. The knife stopped.

"I was born there," she said quietly, her voice almost a whisper. "In a village that no longer exists. The plateau doesn't just conquer—they consume, they erase. Culture. Memory. Magic. My mother… she sang to the trees. The Plateau cut out her tongue. My father… fought. He was turned into one of their branded."

Elric's stomach knotted. "I'm sorry."

Liora looked at him then, really looked. Her expression softened, just slightly. "You're not like most humans."

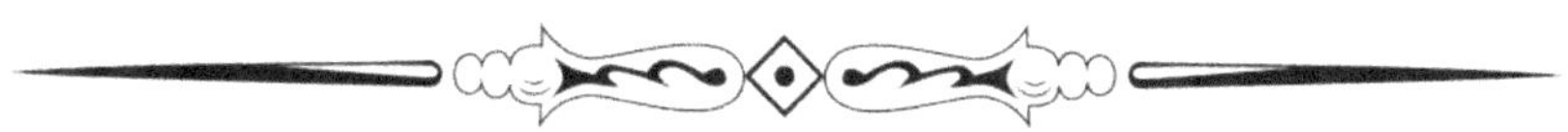

He smiled faintly. "I've been told that before."

Nib stirred, muttering in his sleep. "No flying fish… not again…"

A silence fell—less heavy than before. The kind that meant, maybe, they would all survive the night.

Liora sheathed her blade. "I'll keep watch first."

"Thanks."

They slept in a hollow, faintly sweet-smelling tree under starlight at night.

Liora was honing her twin daggers, Nib Fast asleep next to the fire, and Elric stared up at the stars—hoping that one of them would lead him to his father's whereabouts.

For though he had never been nearer, the truth weighed heavier than ever before.

As Elric stared up at the sky, hoping one of those stars still remembered the path to his father. He had never been closer. And yet, the weight of it had never felt heavier.

The Plateau was near.

And it was watching.

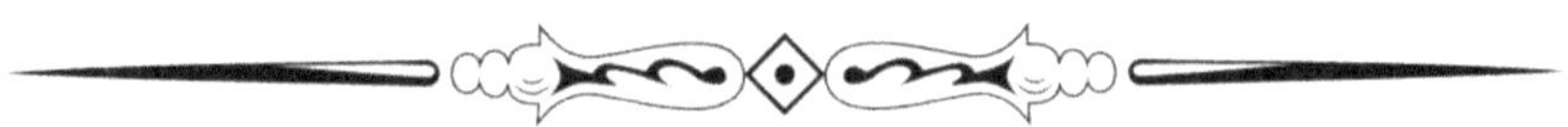

Chapter Eight
Fire in the East

Morning arrives in a dull golden light. In the ruins, the dawn was silent – no birdsong, only the soft wind whispering through the broken chimneys. The air was pale pewter, fogged with weak amber light that fought to seep through stones draped with moss. Elric awoke to smell wet stone and smoke—not fire, but the kind that lingers long after it is extinguished.

Liora stayed along the edge of the square, gazing out onto the horizon. Her bow was slung once more across her shoulder, but her stance hadn't eased. She was a statue of restrained fury.

Nib stretched and rubbed his eyes beneath his helmet. "Mmm. My waffles were dragon-free in my dreams."

"Too bad," Liora answered without deviation. "We have to leave. I do not enjoy the scent of the air."

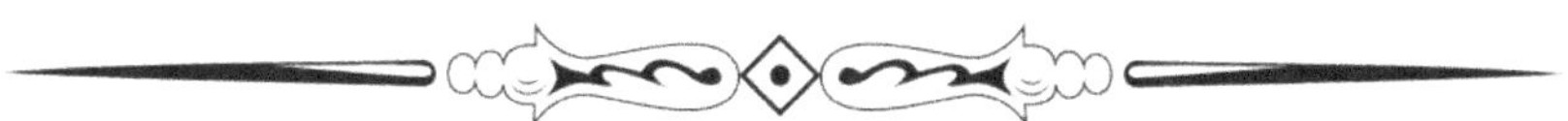

Elric stood, shoving the small pouch in which he had kept the crumpled map. It pulsed once—just barely—like it was stirring with the wind. "You think they're after us?"

Liora nodded. "Maybe. Or maybe the land's just telling us to run."

They moved down the empty street, dilapidated buildings yielding to wild green and sun-streaked paths. The sun, too, seemed wrong this morning, too red, too low.

That's when it happened.

The sky had turned red long before the flames had ever touched the earth. Elric was the first to witness the shimmer on the horizon, as if heat were being drawn from a forge. It spread across the east in a wide band, pulsing like a heart. Then there was the sound—a rumble at first, like the world's throat clearing. It built, cracked, boomed—and the leaves on the trees rustled free.

"Down!" Liora hissed.

They crawled under a thorn bush as the sound grew louder. Nib let out a high-pitched squeak and buried himself within Elric's cloak. "That is not thunder. That is wingbeats."

The first fire blazed across the sky like an arrow of flame. Then another. And another.

They ran.

Through brambles and thorns, down through time-tarnished slopes. The snarl behind them mounted in volume, a chorus of seared lungs and screaming trees. The forest wept, branches cracking as fire swept through the canopy.

A shadow above—so wide it blanketed the sun.

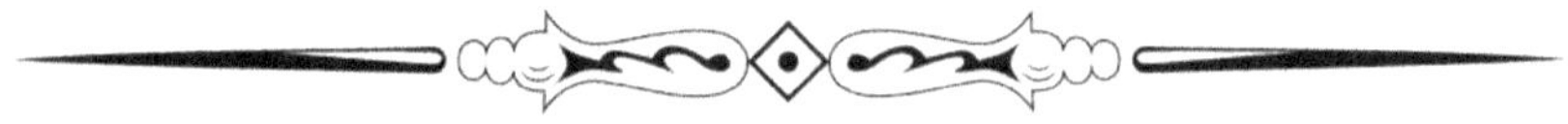

"East Plateau dragon scouts," Liora whispered, her voice strained. "Not just a raid. Clearing something. Hunting something."

Elric felt the wand at his belt pulsing, the runes softly aglow through his arm.

And he knew, deep in the marrow of his bones—they were hunting him.

The sky was red before fire so much as touched the earth.

Elric saw it first, a flash on the horizon, a heat haze off a furnace. It spread wide across the east, pulsing like a heartbeat. Then the noise: initially a rumbling low, like the world's throat clearing its throat. It grew louder, cracked, boomed—and the leaves on the trees shook loose.

"Down!" Liora hissed.

They dodged behind a clump of spiny bushes as the sound increased. Nib shrieked at the pitch of his voice and scurried into Elric's cloak. "That's not thunder. That's wingbeats."

The streak of fire shot across the sky like a molten arrow. Then another. And another.

They ran.

Down through brambles and thorns, slopes churned by time. Behind them, the noise grew into a roar – a wild mix of burning breath and screaming trees. The forest screamed, branches cracking as fire devoured the canopy.

Above, a shadow moved—so wide it cast the sun in shadow.

"East Plateau dragon scouts," Liora gasped, her voice strained. "This isn't a raid. They're clearing something. Searching for something."

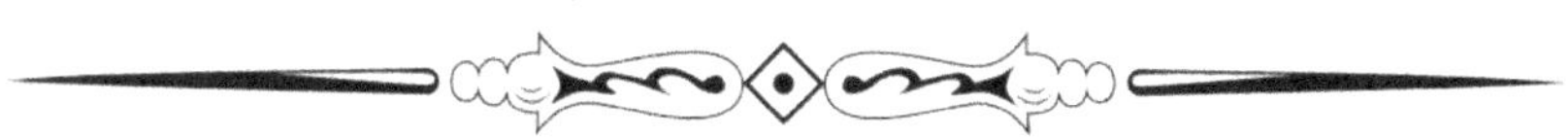

Elric felt the wand in his side vibrating, the runes glowing faintly under his sleeve.

And he knew, in the marrow of his bones—they sought him.

"In the hollow!" Liora shouted.

They dove into a crevice between two giant stone outcroppings, where a cluster of ancient trees clustered in a ring like elderly hags whispering. Nib drew a branch across the entrance as flames popped above. The air was oppressive. Elric's heart thrashed in his chest.

And then, it happened again.

His fingers began to glow.

No magic, no wand, no incantation. Only a throb—an agonizing, searing power that compelled its way through his skin like something trying to escape.

"Elric," Nib growled, taking a step back. "Your fingers are—uh—on fire."

"I didn't do it on purpose!" Elric cried, clutching his hands to his chest. "I have no idea how to make it stop!"

The light intensified orange, then violet. Sparks erupted from his hands. He felt the world spin around him. He could feel the wind bend, feel the air tremble, feel the fire in the sky as if it were inside him.

And then—

Silence fell.

The flames outside faded away.

Something creaked behind them. Gentle, but extremely old.

They turned to look.

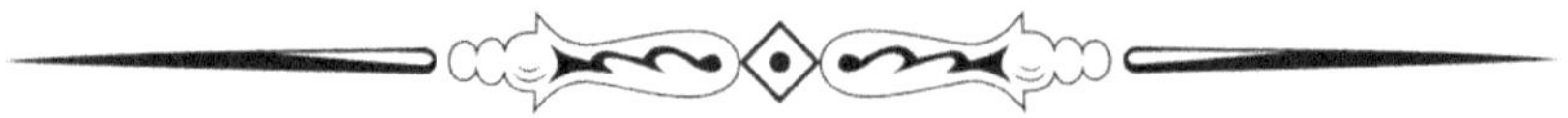

At the entrance stood a figure made of light and bark. A woman, or at least a figure like one—spun from twisting branches and leaves that shone like stars imprisoned in resin. Her eyes were green like moss.

"Son of the flame," she said, voice gentle and leaves-rustling in a storm. "You wield a magic that was buried for a purpose."

Elric stared. "Who are you?"

"A memory," the spirit replied. "A whisper from the Grove. You burn not fire forged by spell, but by soul. It is forbidden not because it is evil. but because it costs."

"Mean?" he breathed, shaking.

"You are burning your own threads to spin something beautiful. And when those threads are used up."

She trailed off.

And vanished among the trees.

Elric sat rigid.

Nib took another step. "I don't care for magic metaphors. They always foreshadow that someone is going to die."

Elric still stared at his hands—peaceful now, but humming. "Why wasn't I warned?"

"I will," Liora snapped.

The others followed her gaze.

She stood up, arms crossed, eyes glowering.

"There's something you should know," she said. "Your father. The war. The Plateau. It's not a matter of land anymore."

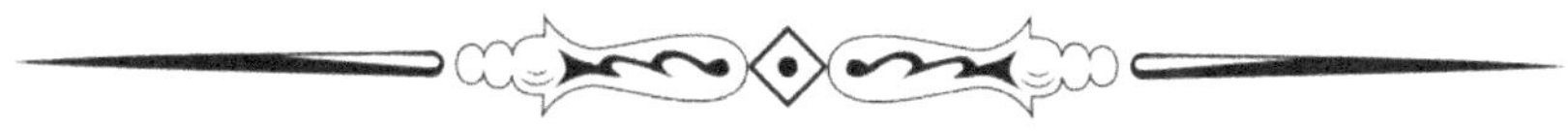

She drew a deep breath.

"Rumors—good ones. The east tribe—they're recruiting people with. unusual talents. Not for ransom. Not for interrogation."

"To hire."

Elric chest tightened. The ground beneath him seemed to shift.

"For what?" he asked instantly.

"A ritual," she breathed, barely more than a whisper. "To awaken something older than the world itself. They think that blood from powerful mages can open a door never to be opened."

Elric's heart dropped to his stomach.

Liora nodded. "Your father didn't vanish. He was kidnapped."

Elric was silent for a long time.

The fire had gone from his hands, but in their place, it had taken root in his chest-a smouldering pain that flared behind his ribs like a lantern in a storm. He thought furiously: we must find his father alive. or worse, kept for something worse than death.

"We have to find him," he said finally.

"We will," said Liora. Her voice was steady, but her eyes held the same fire that burned in Elric. "But we cannot just storm the fortress of the Plateau. We must know what they are doing, when, and where. And we must be more powerful."

"And smarter," said Nib, pulling a leaf out of his ear. "They have dragons. I have a stick and a bag of gooseberries."

Elric found himself smiling. "You also have a fantastically impressive talent for fleeing."

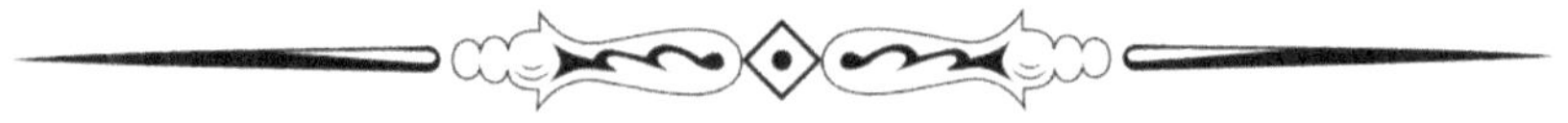

"Thank you. I practice daily."

They crept out of the hollow cautiously. Smoke still brooded in the air, and the dark clouds heavens still churned with soot-dark clouds. But the dragons had driven east, leaving behind them a swath burned bare trees blackened, streams that steamed like they were boiling, and entire glades incinerated down to ash.

As they walked, Elric's thoughts continued to return to the forest spirit's warning. It costs.

He could feel it now more than ever – how the world felt thinner, as though the veil between what was and what could be was coming apart. Every time he'd used his magic lately, he'd felt something within him stretch. And the last time? It had almost snapped.

Liora commented on his silence.

You'll have to learn to control it," she said. "Not just allow it to seep out."

"Do you do that?"

"I make spells. You are the spell. It's not the same."

They passed along the edge of a sunk copse where the trees grew gnarled and writhe-limbed, the trunks twisted like old fists. A single toad opened its eyes on a rock and croaked solemnly, as if to say, You don't belong here.

They didn't stop until the sun was low and they'd reached the edge of an overlook—a rocky bluff that provided view to the far east. From here, they could see it: the faint tendril of smoke that wreathed like a shadow from the edge of the horizon.

The Plateau.

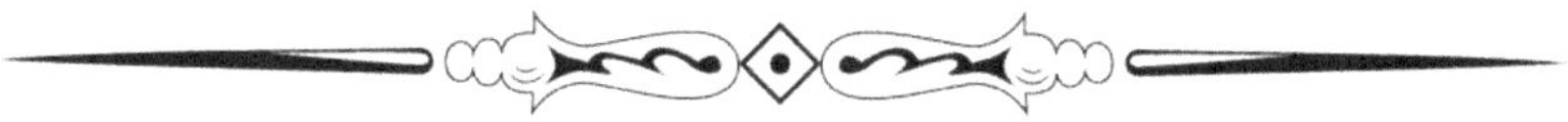

Even from here, it looked wrong. The clouds there took on an unnatural thickness, and lightning split the air silently above in a group of trees that would not sway with the wind.

"That's it," Liora said.

Elric felt a shiver run along the back of his neck. "That's where he is.".

Nib dug into his sack and brought out a rather flattened gooseberry. "Right. So how do we get into the most highly guarded, magically locked, dragon-watched terror in the world without becoming soup?"

"Carefully," Liora said. "And with help."

She turned to Elric. "Tomorrow, we will find the old Wayfinder's lodge in the Whispering Valley. If anyone knows the layout of the Plateau—and how to avoid their wards—it's the mapkeeper who betrayed them years ago."

Elric frowned. "I heard he vanished."

"He did," said Liora. "But I know where to look."

The sky above them faded from gold to deep blue, and the first stars shone—faint sparklings over a land that was shattered, yet lovely. Below them, the fires on the Plateau burned more brightly now, a challenge.

Elric tightened the straps of his pack.

He would walk into the darkness. He would follow the fire. And he would find his father—at any price.

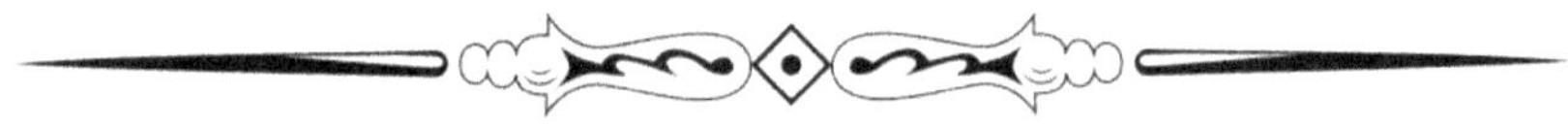

Chapter Nine
The Hollow Map

It was raining whispers.

Not really rain, but the sort which fell in the Whispering Valley—soft murmurings that came from all the trees, the rocks, even the grass stalks, as if the earth itself were having a faraway conversation. Some claimed that the whispers were memories, trapped in the roots of the land. Others claimed that they were deceptions, planted by the Plateau to deceive wayfarers.

Nib, naturally, had a different version.

"They're just nosy spirits," he complained, grasping the hem of Elric's cloak as they proceeded cautiously down the slippery path. "Most probably criticizing our boots and asking why I only brought three socks."

Elric chuckled tiredly, but his gaze never softened. There was something in this valley that waited. The atmosphere was thick where it ought to be light, the sun dimming despite still being morning. Trees

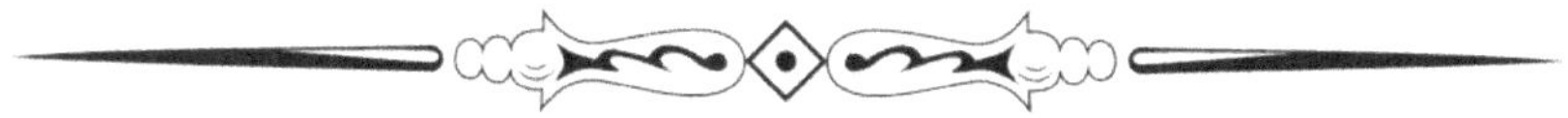

bent overhead like cathedral vaults, their trunks were dark ink, smeared with shiny moss. Distantly, a low beat was audible—a slow, patient heartbeat like the heart of a creature too large for any single creature to call its own.

"Stay on the path," Liora cautioned, her bow drawn and ready. "The valley does not take kindly to wandering feet."

"How does a valley dislike something?" Nib complained.

"It recalls trespass. And it bites."

They trudged for hours until the forest swung open into an eye-shaped clearing. In the center, coiled among roots and rock outcroppings, was a ruined stone lodge—almost consumed by ivy and mist.

Elric walked cautiously. The lodge was ancient, older than any ruin he'd ever walked through, but its door was still intact: white wood with serpentine, star, and one eye carving that seemed to follow them as they moved toward it.

"Are you sure this is the place?" Elric asked.

Liora nodded. "The Hollow Mapkeeper once resided here. If his map still lives, it'll be inside."

"And if he's still in there?" Nib asked, voice trembling.

"Then we ask nicely. Very, very nicely."

Elric knocked and stepped back.

There was silence. No reply.

Then—click—the door creaked open on its own.

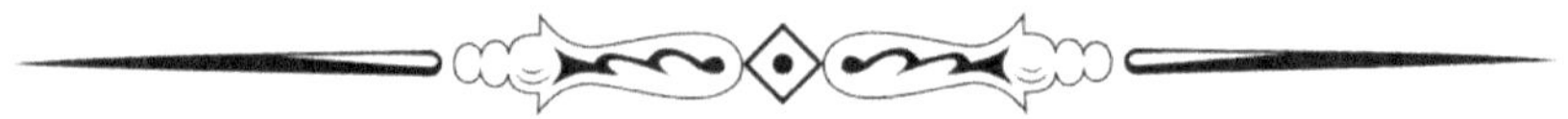

The air within reeked of dust, ink, and years. Scrolls cluttered wooden tables, some smoldering half-way, others curled up like dead leaves. A single candle floated in mid-air, nervously wavering. Shadows moved on the walls, coalescing into shapes that writhed like memories trying to form.

In the center of the room stood a pedestal, and on top of it... a map.

It glowed faintly, not with light, but with intent—like it was waiting.

Elric approached it, heart racing. Before them on the map lay the Plateau, but differently than before. It was an old map, full of arcane symbols and curving lines like pen-rivers. As his hand reached out, the air grew cold. Shadows on the wall stopped their moving.

"I would not touch it," a voice said behind them.

They turned around.

An old man stood at the far end of the room, swathed in a cloak of stars and feathers. His eyes were colorless; his face creased with ink as if he had been tattooed with entire pages of forgotten lore. He wore no sword—only a twisted staff made of bone and thorn.

"You're the mapkeeper," Elric stated.

"I was," the man replied. "Now I'm the keeper of consequences."

He took another step closer. "You seek the path into the Plateau. I can see it in your bones. I can see it in your flame."

"Do you know where father is?" Elric, with his voice taut like an overstrained thread, asked.

The old man chose not to answer quickly. The cloudy eyes—yet not at all blind—sparked with a glimmered expression that bore no meaning

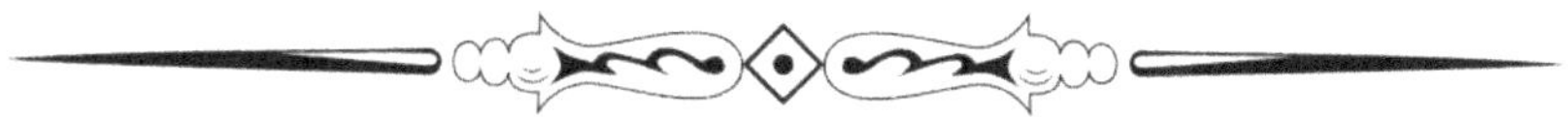

and went unread. He leaned in; the smell of pine smoke and mildew permeated his cloak.

"I know where your path begins, boy," he said slowly, his words dropped in the still water of the other. "But the question is... do you truly wish to walk it?"

Elric gazed downward. Between them, the map had ceased being simply ink upon parchment; it gave forth a faint glow in the shack's dimness. Light sifted through the warped wooden slats, crookedly beaming above, catching on dust motes akin to falling stars. The map gave a single pulse under his fingers as if it were alive. It was longing for him.

The tightness squeezed that boyish throat as his mind jerked between images of his father-wavering voice, smiling face, and bright morning when he had ridden away-to the fear now building up in his chest.

The wind moaned outside through broken shingles. Silence resounded inside, as though it was holding its breath.

But there was no stopping him now.

A deep breath, seasoned with the smelling note of old ash and moss, went through him as he kept his hand basking on that glowing edge.

"Yes," he whispered.

Softly flared the map, then dimmed down to embers on a hearth, as if it, too, had been waiting a long time to be chosen.

The mapkeeper nodded, slow and somber. "Then the map is yours. But heed this—once in hand, never to be given back. It will guide you, but it will guide them to you."

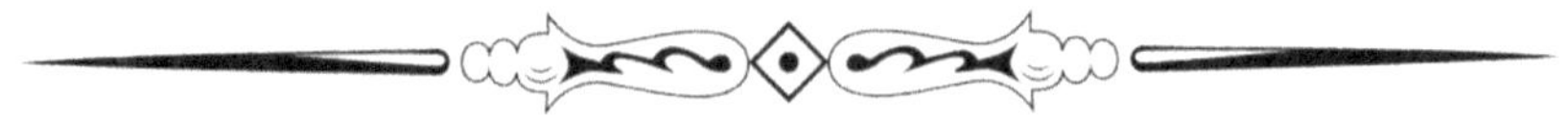

Before Elric could ask them who they were, the map folded up, floating into his hands. The room darkened. The shadows whispered again, but this time they said one word—clear, cold, and absolute.

"Run."

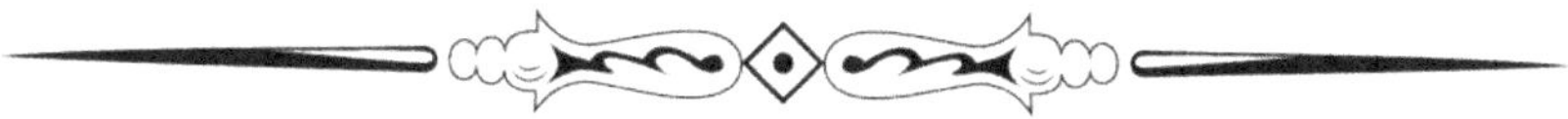

Chapter Ten

The Watchers of the East

The route through the East had not appeared on any map that Elric had ever seen, not even the Hollow Map, presently crowded with curious symbols he didn't understand but sensed in his bones. As if the road only revealed itself when the world itself deemed worthy—or doomed—to walk it.

Heavy fogs wrapped around the turning road, curling around pointed black pines that grew sharper than they had any need to. Nib perched on Elric's shoulder, surprisingly quiet, except for the occasional nervous hum. Liora, hood low over silver-blonde hair, had taken the lead. She walked as if each step was a challenge she dared the Plateau to meet.

"Elric," she said in a sharp tone, not turning around. "Can you feel it?"

Elric did. The air grew thick, filled with looking. Not the careful quiet that forest imposed upon holding breath held, but other—the deliberate

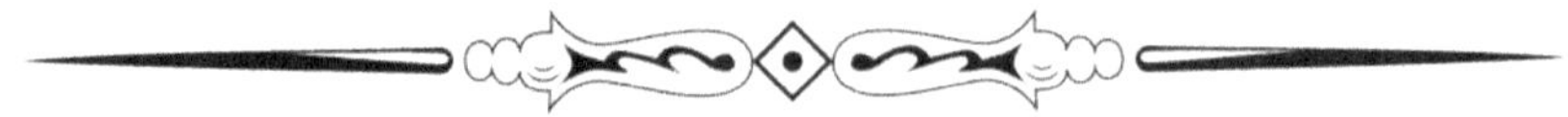

sort, clever sort. It tickled in the back of his head and made the fire-wand strapped to side sizzling hot.

And the wind ceased.

And a voice—more than a voice, dozens of them—whispered over mist.

"Turn back, child of fire. This way is not for you."

Liora's breath caught. "Watchers," she whispered, her voice barely audible. "They stand guard over the Eastern gateway. Ancient guardians corrupted to become spies."

Out of the mist, shapes solidified—tall, hooded silhouettes, neither quite shadow nor substance. Their faces were hidden behind silver masks that displayed runes that seemed to flicker in and out of being. Each carried a stuff of darkened wood topped with a pale, glowing orb.

One of them defied ranks, its form barely visible in the swirling mist around it. It moved like a wave on water—half-dark, half-metal, eyes blazing like coals underwater.

"You carry magic not your own," it said, voice neither high nor low, but vibrating as though sucked out of the water. "You carry the fire of the forbidden spring."

Elric's throat tightened. He could feel the pressure of the fire-wand against his hip—warm now, as if it had stirred from slumber. But he stood resolute against the Watcher's stare and moved forward.

"I did not take it," he lied, the pulse in his ears deafening. "But I will not give it up."

The Watcher tilted its head on a groan like aged wood. "The Plateau already beckons to you. You hold the regard of the Unseen Flame."

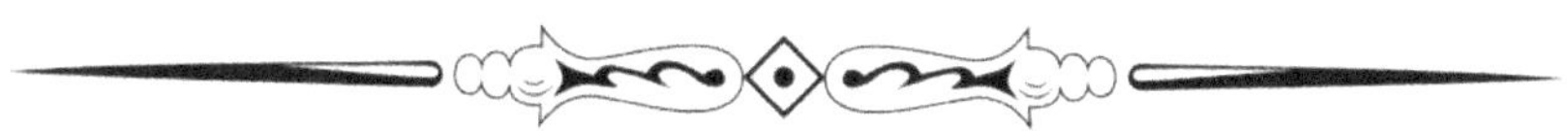

The wand blazed in its sheath at that. Heat spilled off it like breath on glass—ravenous, ancient, irresistible. Elric's hand spasmed at his hip. He could sense it calling, not in voice, but in hunger.

Liora moved forward to get between him and the group. Her cloak fluttered behind her as if she was in a wind that no one else could feel. "We're just passing through," she told him, voice as cold as steel. "Move aside."

The Watchers didn't flinch. The fog in the circle thickened, becoming dense and opaque—like churning smoke. "The Warlord of Emberspire has spoken—all flame-born shall be brought to his tower. You will go with us."

"No, thank you!" Nib piped up from Elric's shoulder, his fur standing on end, his tail quivering. "We already have quite enough appalling fates planned out for the day!"

A whip-quick motion. The leading Watcher raised its staff, and tendrils of spirit-magic light unfolded from its tip, coiling like supernatural vines. They spat towards the company.

Elric didn't respond. He responded.

The flame-wand leapt into his hand, its sigils afire. Red light flared like the sun breaking storm clouds. Crash of sound, below, it burst outward in a surge of blinding power. The fog burst apart with screaming wisps of a thousand. Two Watchers were knocked reeling back, bursting into trees with a report of shattering glass.

Elric gasped knees shaking, the wand heavy in his hand like scalding iron. He had not meant to unleash that amount of power.

It took itself.

"It's hungry," he panted, breath snagging.

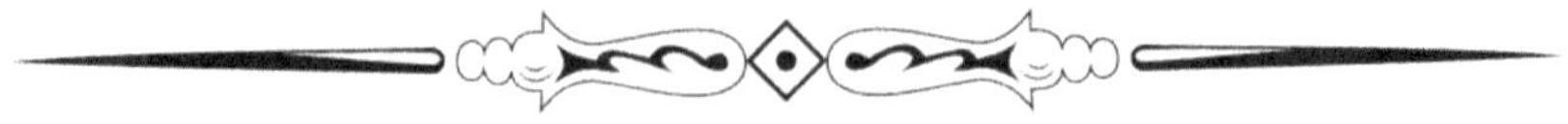

Liora threw an arm around him, steadying him with a firm grip. Her eyes blazed—not with fear, but fury. "You shouldn't have done it," she gritted through clenched teeth. "Now they'll pursue us. All of them."

"I had to," Elric panted. "They'd have marched us to the Plateau in shackles."

A distant, unhuman horn blew in the mist, long and low, like the call of something ancient rousing.

Backwards, the shattered fog began to re-form, curling as wounded smoke around the figures that were being left behind.

The Watchers were reformed, their masks splintering with light. But they hadn't time to strike again before a colossal horn blasted across the mountains—low, long, and terrible. The Watchers froze, listening.

"They are called," one muttered, running back into the fog. "You are lucky, Flameborn."

And so instantaneously, they vanished, melting into mist like breath on glass.

Elric collapsed to his knees, chest heaving. The wand trembled in his grip, glowing still. He dropped it. For a moment, it didn't go out.

Nib picked it up carefully. "You're getting too strong, Elric. Magic's not a toy anymore."

"I know," Elric whispered. "But we're running out of time."

They spent the night under a rock outcropping in the shape of a roaring beast. The heavens above were copper-colored and otherworldly bruises in the sky. Elric gazed at the Hollow Map as it reconfigured, the next stop softly glowing: a tower of darkness encircled by strands of silver light.

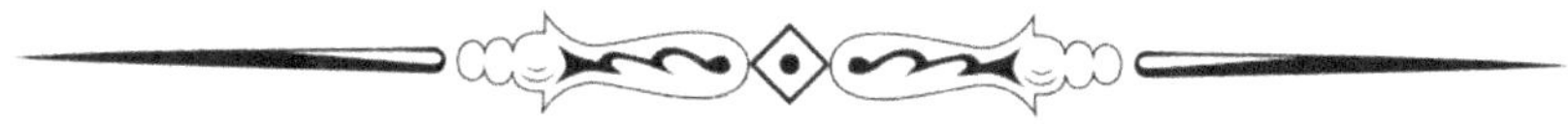

Liora looked over his shoulder. "The Tower of Threads," she snarled. "There they keep what they hold most precious… and most dangerous."

Elric did not speak. In his mind, a voice other than his own spoke from the wand:

"Memory for magic. Flame for freedom."

And deep down in his heart, a part of him already knew: the price would be paid soon enough.

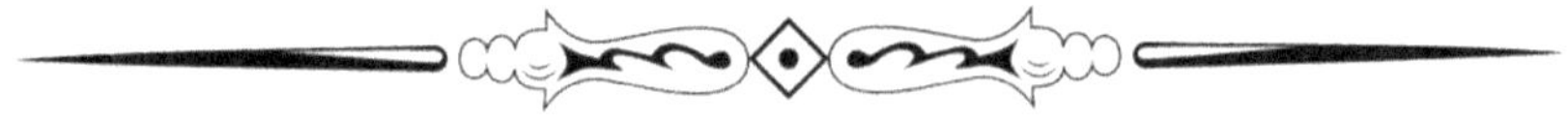

Chapter Eleven
Into the Plateau

They climbed to the rim of the Eastern Plateau at dawn, where mountains splintered like broken bone and steel-blue sky glared down. A high, arcing road wound up onto the cliffs, dotted with waystations and sentinel towers that flared with torches.

From this height, Elric could see the vast stretch of land beyond—ashen fields, towns scorched and silent, and the black silhouettes of war machines crawling across the plains like beetles. The Plateau was a land at war with itself.

Liora wrapped a worn scarf around Elric's head, tucking in his fire-marked hair. "You're a merchant's apprentice now," she said. "Quiet. Limp a little. Look bored."

"Bored?" Elric echoed.

"Nothing's more suspicious than a boy trying not to look suspicious."

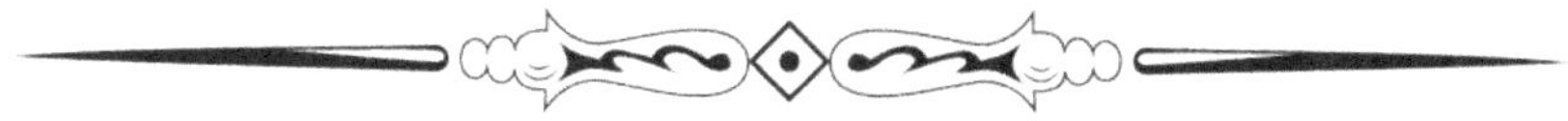

"And me?" Nib chimed in, hopping out from Elric's satchel.

"You're the family pet." No talking. If they ask, you're a very ugly squirrel."

"I am not—" But Liora shot him a look, and he zipped his mouth shut with a tiny imaginary key.

They fell in with a caravan of ragged merchants—hulking figures in patchwork cloaks, their carts groaning under burdens of spiceroot, coils of rusty wire, and cages full of flapping swamphens. Their faces were created by the sun and wary, but they all stayed silent. All of them pledged their heads as they rode toward the checkpoint.

Elric pulled his hood down. Nib hid deep in his satchel. Liora pulled a scarf across her face and shifted her stance like a shadow changing shape.

The gates before loomed—iron-banded and wide, mounted between two stone towers carved with ancient sigils. There was the sigil of the Warlord's dominion: a golden flame on deep crimson, banners streaming in the gusting wind like lips of fire.

A line of Plateau guards stood on either side of the gate. Their armor was shiny obsidian, edges as jagged as volcanic glass. Visors glinted in the sky's reflection, revealing nothing below. Even their breathing came from grates carved in snarling animal patterns.

One of them stepped forward, a jagged pike diagonally across his chest, and let out a low, guttural growl.

"Wait."

The caravan stopped.

The eyes swept the group like a searchlight sweeps over scattered leaves. The voice was oil on grit. "Papers."

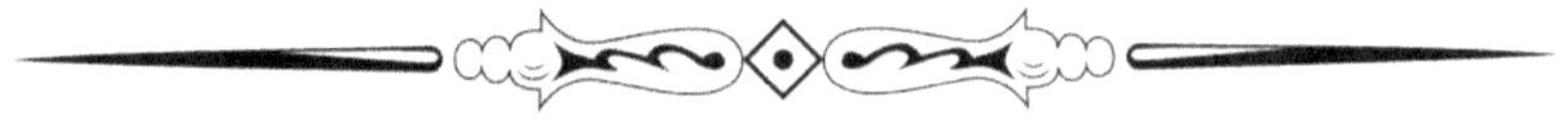

The head trader, an ancient woman with a crooked back and metal spits in her cheeks, held out a shaken sheaf of parchment. He scanned it—then pointed a gauntleted finger at Elric's group.

"You. Red scarf Man

Elric's heart hammered. Nib already was muttering something that sounded darn close to "bad, bad, very bad."

Liora's hand found her belt.

But before anger could erupt, the old trader spat a rough laugh. "She traded me for it in Thornmarket. Bottle of bluefire ink, rare stuff. You think I'd sell silk to a daughter of the Flame?"

The guard tilted his head. Another tick passed.

Liora stood firmly.

Elric's throat dusted.

The guard stepped closer, visor flashing with a distorted image of Elric's face. "That scarf has silk forged from the Plateau. Only scions and soldiers use that."

He Ask, "Purpose of visit?"

"Delivery of metalwork. Clients Duskgate."

The guard regarded Elric, squinting. "The boy ill?"

"Healer said it's swamp-fever," Liora spoke quickly. "Not catching. Just hideous."

The guard smiled, returned the scroll, and waved them past.

Then he growled again. "Move on.".

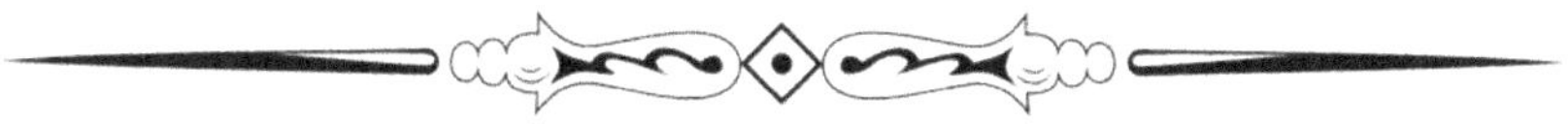

The gates creaked open to the moan of giants. The caravan jolted forward, the guards watching them like wolves on a bottleneck.

Elric exhaled a lungful of air he hadn't known he'd been holding.

They were inside.

But behind them, the mirrored visors continued to shine—watching. Waiting.

Within the Plateau's walls, the brutality could not be concealed—only a cautious dance of silence regarding it.

They proceeded through charred avenues where ash did not fall but seemed to settle, never accumulating, never disappearing. Skeletal children crouched beside shattered fountains, cleaning stonework covered in soot and rot, their vacant eyes unnervingly wide. A boy, no taller than Elric's waist, scraped moss from cracked tiles with the tip of a spoon.

Chains clanked out in rhythm behind them—women and men yoked like oxen to iron wagons filled with sun-baked bricks, their bodies bruised and coated in dust. None glanced at them. None was foolish enough.

Above, red pennants streamed from balcony spikes, emblazoned with the golden sigil of Emberspire's flame. Watchtowers lined every major crossing, archers residing them like statues, still but never sightless.

Liora slumped down, hands stuffed into her pockets. Nib did not even tremble deep in the folds of Elric's cloak.

Even strangers were the lanterns. Hung from gilt poles or floating on spindly silver chains, they burned with an immobile flame—a corpse blue or starving white, flickering without a quiver. Their light never gave

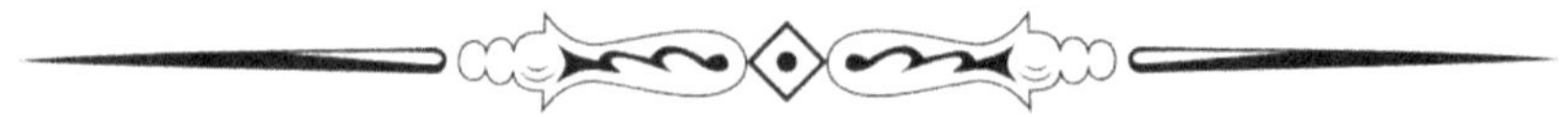

off heat. Their power pulsed unnaturally, as if something inside them breathed without lungs.

"What burns them?" Elric whispered.

Liora didn't answer. Her jaw was clenched too tightly.

He looked up at one of the lanterns above—something moving behind its glow. A formless shadow, twisting like the smoke within a glass jar.

Ill magic.

Two guards passed by them, dragging along a man babbling behind the barbed glass collar. Blood ran down his neck, into his tunic.

Elric veered away.

And still the city existed, as if unaware that it was sick. Above, the sky was thin, rusty, and misty, as though it had forgotten how to be blue.

"Why are they all so faded?" Elric panted.

Liora's gaze stayed ahead. "The Plateau doesn't fight wars. It sucks the life out of people. Each spell they use drains from someone else's memories, dreams, even names. That's why your father is alive."

Elric turned on her. "What are you telling me?"

She paused and pulled him into an alley where they wouldn't be heard. "If your father is fire-touched like you, they wouldn't kill him. They'd exploit him. For magic."

Elric sensed the vibration of the fire-wand against his ribs, a warning beat in his side. "Then we're not moving anywhere until we locate him."

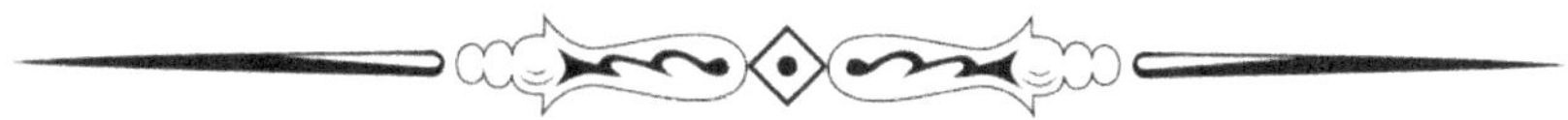

Liora nodded. "There's a fortress near the heart of the city—built into the ruins of the old star temple. It's where they keep prisoners of war, especially those with magical blood."

"And it's guarded?

"Protected by a dragon as gold is. But even dragons don't know the temple tunnels better than I do."

Elric gazed at her, astounded. "Why?"

She faced away. "Because I was supposed to die there."

A horn sounded in the distance. Not a war horn—but something strange. Higher. As if wind were whistling through the world's bones.

And in the distance, the sky above the tower glowed, as if the stars themselves were trying to wink in the daylight.

"The Tower of Threads," Liora whispered. "Where they pull their magic and where they'll suck your father dry."

Elric swallowed hard, his resolve firming.

"Then we go tonight."

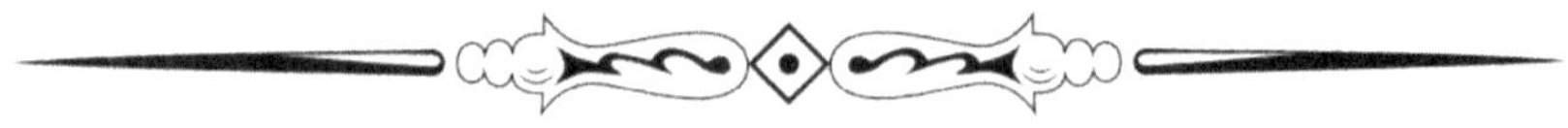

Chapter Twelve
The Tower of Threads

They rode at midnight.

Liora led them through corkscrew alleys and tunnels hidden beneath rusting drains and piles of shattered stone. The air was thick with the stench of damp earth and iron. Nib rode silently on Elric's shoulder, his usual chatter clamped shut — as if even feared the stones might be listening.

"The temple was once a star-gazer's sanctuary," Liora panted, cradling a flaring light-crystal in her palm. "A sanctuary of hope. It's now. warped. The Plateau corrupted it to harness dream-magic. They call it the Tower of Threads, because they spin energy from memory, knitting it into spells.".

Elric said nothing. His mind burned with the image of his father—Calwen, brave and charred by fire, who told stories by candlelight and wore soot on his arms like badges. The man who had vanished when war marched east. The man Elric had gone to save.

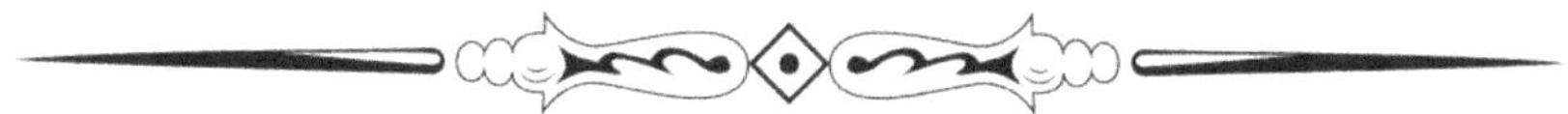

They reached a half-eaten grate, choked with vines. Liora crouched inside first, then gestured them to follow. Below, a stairway bent into the earth, lit by strands of blue light that danced like cobwebs.

And at the bottom stood a door of black stone, locked with runes that pulsed with magic so old even Nib winced.

"Wards," growled Nib. "They're listening."

"Not for long." Elric replied. He stepped forward and drew the fire-wand. It blazed in his hand, not with flame—but with memory.

He let it guide him.

Let the magic drink in the moment when he had first spoken beneath the whispering trees, leaves spinning around like quiet applause, the world yawned open in gasping wonder. Let it taste the scent of damp still, woodsmoke, the thrill in his fingertips when light had answered him, alive and obedient.

And deeper still — he offered it laughter. His father's. Afternoon in the yard, pounding bent nails into weathered wood, building a crooked birdhouse that listed to one side. Sawdust floated in sunbeams golden as honey. His father's calloused hands over him. The groan of a story half-told. The warmth of a world that had not yet broken.

The last day of peace before the war.

And in letting it declare these things—he felt the weight of their change. Not to go away. Not to forget. But hammered into something denser, brighter, and far more lethal.

The wand glowed gold and struck the door like a key.

The runes burst—then shattered into dust.

They entered the tower.

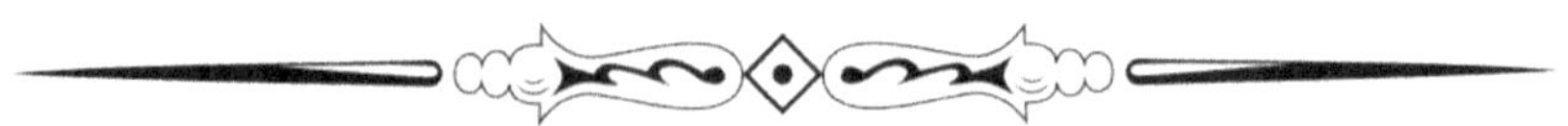

Strings of light drifted in the air like strands of silvery silk, each one glowing with moments in a person's life. A girl scattering dandelions. A soldier home from war. A boy and his father were on a lake.

Elric reached out for one—but Liora caught his wrist.

"Don't touch them. They feed on memories. One negative thought and you'll forget who you are."

They ascended the corkscrew staircase, its stepped stone surfaces smoothed hollow by grief and time.

It got progressively worse at each level.

The others held glass cases—scores—piled against the walls like trophies. Within each, hopes glowed in artificial suspension: a girl's laugh beneath snow, a field of golden wheat, a child running to arms that would never open again. Elric paused, breath fogging the glass of one case. The dream pulsed weakly, as if it remembered being real.

At the next level down, cells spilled into the darkness. In each, prisoners sat hunched and unseeing, jaws moving in slow, hopeless repetition. Names. Names they couldn't decide were their own or someone else's. A prayer of lost selves.

A shiver seeped into Elric's bones, an awe too deep to speak.

Nib grasped the back of his collar with both paws now, his customary sass silenced. "This is bad," he breathed. "It devours what makes you. you."

Nonetheless, they ascended.

The steps gave way to a network of curving paths—no longer linear but woven together like the very strands for which the tower was better known. The three crept slowly, their breathing thin, as though each step carried with it the weight of memory and magic.

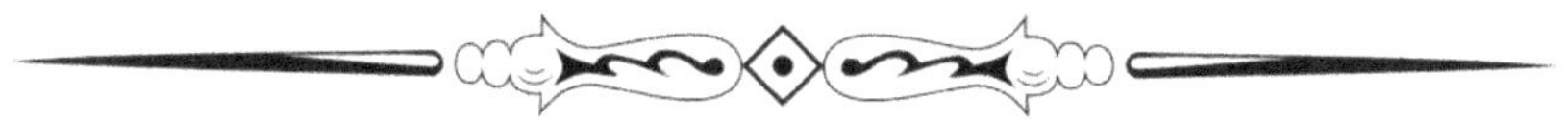

Room of Echoes

The first door groaned open on a sigh that seemed to whisper Elric's name.

Inside, nothing moved—yet the air buzzed like a distant hum. The room was circular; walls etched with runes that flickered softly. As they stepped inside, voices rose.

But not just any voices.

"Where were you?" came a cry—his mother's, trembling and desperate.

"Promise me you'll come back," his own voice pleaded, years younger.

"No!" Liora cried out beside him, rubbing her temples. Her own past overwhelmed her—tears of a brother lost to flames, wails of betrayal. She stumbled, almost falling.

Nib screamed, spun around in mid-air. "Shut up shut up SHUT UP!"

The room feasted on their regret. For every step they took trying to move ahead, regrets slithered down their legs like ivy.

Elric's teeth gritted, he raised his wand—and rather than fire, this time a blast of noise erupted outward. The echoes crackled like breaking glass, and the door in front of them creaked open.

The Hall of Threads

Threads of gold and black thread hung from the ceiling here like sloppy spiderwebs. Each one hummed softly, vibrating with near-contained power.

Liora reached to move one aside—and vanished.

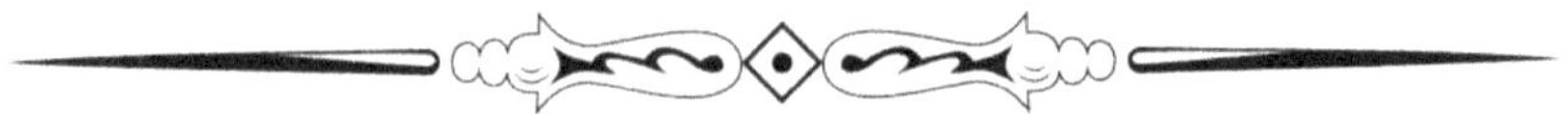

"Liora!" Elric cried, dashing forward.

She was there – her body frozen, eyes wild with fear.

"She's trapped in a memory thread," Nib gasped. "Grab the wrong one and it traps you in your past. Forever, if you're not careful."

Elric's heart pounded.

He moved one by one down the corridor, his wand casting clouds of pale light as he searched the threads. Each held vignettes in the shape of windows—his father instructing him with wooden swords, his own first flash of magic, his mother singing on the porch…

Temptation flayed him. Stay. Remember.

He clenched his teeth, found the thread that pulsed with Liora's aura—and severed it.

She staggered, gasping. "Don't touch anything," she rasped, and they moved on.

The Chamber of the Mirror Flame

A mirrored room. Hundreds, slanted so that the group was reflected thousands of times—tired, shaken, and scarred.

In the center: a flame, floating, contained within a glass sphere.

"Looks safe enough," Nib whispered.

It wasn't.

The moment Elric stepped forward, his reflection twisted. They all distorted. Copies of themselves emerged from each one—Elrics twisted with rage, Lioras in darkness, Nibs with eyes as empty as holes.

They attacked, swift and lethal, the same magic, the same swords.

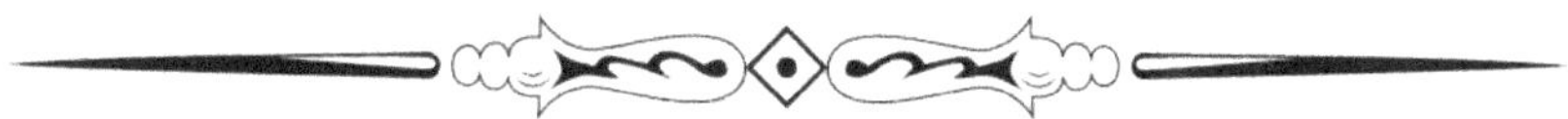

"We're fighting what we could become," Liora bellowed, parrying a strike from her shadow self. "What could we have been!"

Elric understood then: this room tested their resolve.

He closed his eyes amidst chaos. He remembered who he was—not the Plateau's boy of fear or the forest's hunted one—but the son who chose hope.

When he opened his eyes, he raised the wand and whispered, "I chose my path."

Light flared from him, not from fire or flame—but from knowledge.

The forms of the mirror shattered. The sphere broke. The path opened.

The ascent was interminable.

Each Tower ride spiralled like a nightmare sequence. The walls pulsed tenuously, veins of glowing fibre accenting the stone as if arteries of memory. Whispers hailed down the stairways—sometimes whispering Elric's name, sometimes sobbing, sometimes laughing with a sound that caused Nib to shiver and rake claws across Elric's shoulder.

They arrived at a glassy obsidian-hewn hallway illuminated by the faint glow of distant memory-flames suspended above like jellyfish suspended. Each door was stranger than the last.

One room displayed lines of frozen soldiers—soldiers in motion frozen, faces half-obliterated, trapped in glass case. Another held a garden of white roses growing out of skeletal hands. One room contained only feathers that rustled with each breath.

"What is this place?" Liora snarled, swords uncovered but drawn low.

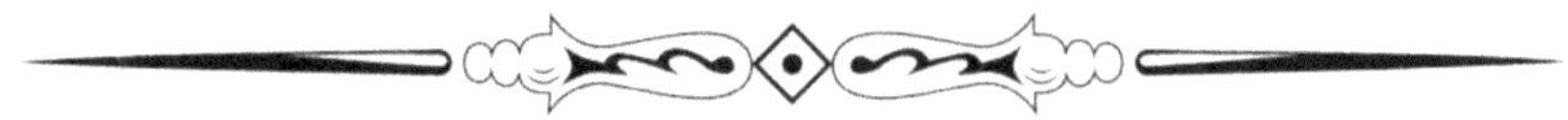

Nib yanked at Elric's hair. "Memory, maybe? Prison of mind? I hate it. I hate it much."

Then they heard it.

A low humming sound - unbroken, rhythmic, as if some vast and ancient thing were whirling near at hand. Elric felt his wand warm against his side. The map in his pocket glowed once, then crumbled to ash. Its task, clearly, was done.

They continued.

There stood a great arched door before them, runes twisting and glowing if one looked at them too hard. Over it was etched in fine gold a word in a long-forgotten tongue. Liora looked at it and furrowed her brow. "I think it says, Here, lie the threads of kings."

Elric extended his hand. The door was warm to his touch.

With a creak that shook the entire floor, it opened inward.

The room beyond was vast—a cathedral, not a room, with the stone spires reaching up into the darkness. There was a loom at the center, as big as any tree, its obsidian and bone frame, the threads of light and shadow that ran through it writhing as if it lived.

And underneath, at its foot, a dais.

Stone and metal, rimmed in runes that squirmed like caught insects.

A figure on it—bound with glimmering cords, head bowed, locks spilling from his temples to the center of the Loom.

Elric stood still. His lips went dry.

"Father," he gasped.

They found him.

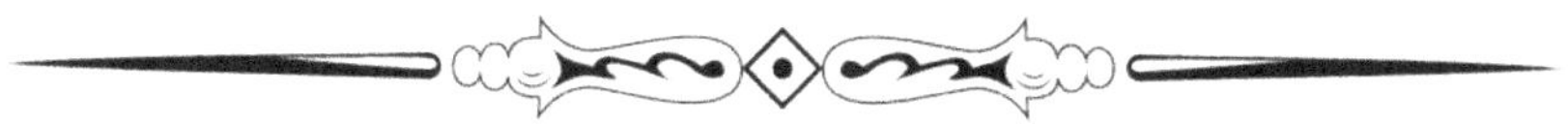

Calwen.

He was bound to a dais of stone and metal; the surface etched in living runes that shimmered and crawled like insects. Thin filaments of golden thread streamed from his temples—memories, pulled slowly and endlessly, winding into the massive loom behind him. The loom pulsed with the colors of thought: flickers of flame, echoes of laughter, battle cries smothered by time.

Elric stumbled forward. "Father…"

Calwen's eyes fluttered, cracked open only slightly slitted like a man on the edge of sleep, or death. His lips trembled with a word, but no sound came. Each thread drawn from him left him dimmer, emptier.

Liora touched Elric's arm, her voice low with wonder and grief. "He lives…"

"But not for long," came a voice like wind through dry parchment.

They spun.

A figure emerged from the shadows, gliding rather than walking. It was tall, inhumanly so, her face looked like pale paper folded too many times—creases and angles that should not be. Her robes shimmered with embroidered fragments: dancing children, crumbling towers, flickers of firelight and shadowed forests.

A Threadbinder.

"Your intrusion was noted the moment you touched the Tower's path," she said, her voice layered as though many versions of her were speaking in harmony, past and future selves entangled.

"Let him go," Elric said, stepping in front of the others. The fire-wand burned against his side, pulsing with the heat of rising fury.

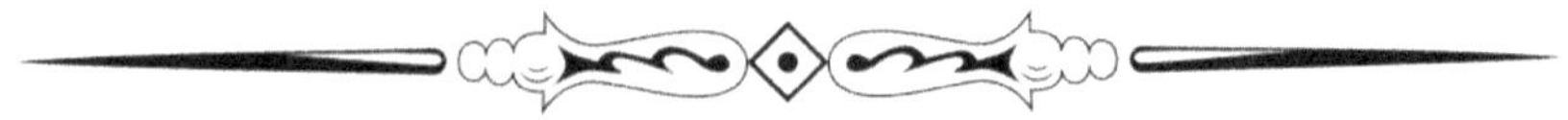

The Threadbinder tilted her head. "Why should I? He feeds the Loom. He is useful."

"He's, my father!"

"And once," she mused, "he was something far greater than that. Hero. Traitor. Seeker. He came here willingly, boy. He gave himself to the Threads."

Elric's heart twisted. "That's a lie."

"Is it?" Her eyes—black pits with pinpricks of gold—glinted. "Then perhaps he should tell you."

She raised one long, spindled hand.

Calwen jerked against his bindings. His eyes snapped open, fully now, glowing faintly with threads not his own.

"Elric…" His voice was raw and rasping. "You shouldn't have come."

Elric stepped forward, confusion and pain warring in his chest. "Why? Why did you leave?"

The Threadbinder sighed, not unkindly. "You may have your answers, little flame born. But they will burn."

She raised her other hand—and the Loom behind Calwen began to shudder. The threads accelerated. The floor cracked with light. Magic, old and bitter, surged like a tidal wave.

Nib squeaked. "Uh-oh. Big loom tantrum."

Liora drew her blades. "We need a plan."

Elric's grip tightened on the wand. No more running.

"I'll face her," he said. "Get my father out.

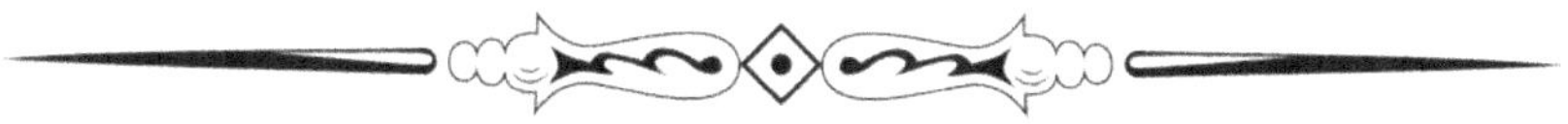

The wand erupted into flame—not destructive, but golden and warm, like light from a fire kept during the long night. The runes on his arms shimmered to life.

And the Threadbinder laughed.

"Then let the unweaving begin." she cooed. "Fire-marked, just like him. You'll make a fine heir to the weave."

"I'm not yours," Elric growled.

The wand leapt to his hand. Flames erupted—but the Binder countered with shadowthreads, wrapping them around his arms, digging into his thoughts. He could feel them pulling—trying to steal the memory he held dearest.

The wand blazed brighter, fire climbing Elric's arm like a tendril, but the Binder's threads were swifter—cold, slick as oil, winding around his wrists, his mind, his memories. They sliced deeper than agony, insinuating themselves into thoughts he hadn't touched in years.

"Elric!" Calwen's cry tore the room apart, wild and despairing. The glittering threads were pulling him dry, sucking splinters of his soul upward into the Loom above. "

But Elric staggered beneath the weight of the shadowthreads. The Tower took a toll as always.

He could feel it: the Weave was brittle now. Fraying. And something in the walls trembled at the ferocity of his fire.

It took something sacred to shatter.

He closed his eyes.

He gave it up.

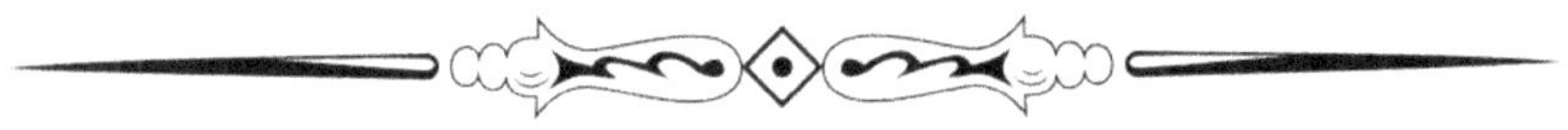

The sun-kissed image wavered to life on the surface of his eyelids: a lake at dusk. The water stilled to glass. His father's hands, calloused and strong, guiding his own small fingers on the fishing rod. Calwen's laughter, rich and real, echoing from the trees like a lullaby made of light.

He released it.

The memory was torn free—not destroyed but offered. A burning surge of heat, then hollow chill in his chest. The tower reacted with a scream.

A convulsion tore through the Weave. The strands twisted, spat—some broke, some flared like paper in the wind.

The Binder screamed, a sound of tearing parchment and cracking ice, stumbling backward as fire and fragmented memory lashed the air. Her robe caught fire—embered threads twisting and devouring themselves. She dispersed into smoke and quiet.

Elric collapsed to one knee, panting, wand still burning in his hand but dwindling.

Calwen inhaled, and the chains fell from him like dead vines.

"Elric…" he whispered, arms shaking outwards.

Elric barely had time to ponder over when the Tower itself groaned low, ancient rumble like stone grieving its own fall.

Liora drew her sword. "Something is coming."

Nib climbed up Elric's back, ears spreading wildly. "I hear boots. Heavy boots."

The walls felt dilapidated.

A section of the room peeled away—not like a door, but like a wound—revealing a coil of dark stone, lit by torches that threw chilly

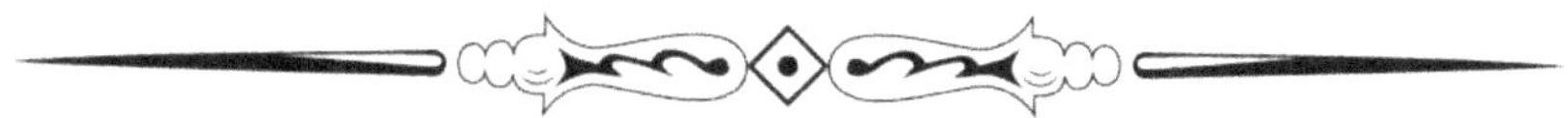

green shadows. Down from its rim stepped a figure wearing obsidian armor, his helmet in the form of a dragon's mouth.

The Warlord of Emberspire.

No visible sword did he wore, but his shadow preceded him like a living creature—twisting, snarling, chasing.

"You set my Binder on fire," he declared, voice as smooth as poison. "And yet you think you can walk away."

Calwen tried to stand, his legs folding under him like a piece of cloth.

Elric stood over him, wand raised, fires dancing through his blood. "I do not fear you."

The warlord didn't blink.

"No. But you should."

His shadow advanced as if to attack.

Liora hurled a knife—he caught it out of the air and extinguished it to embers.

Run, Calwen hacked. "Elric, run! This building's alive, it won't let us out by the same door!"

The Tower lurched violently now, throwing ancient jars off shelves, breaking loose memories from the air. They fluttered like broken feathers, disintegrating in fire.

"Out's by the collapse tunnels!" Nib screamed, pointing her finger toward a side wall where cracks had appeared in the stone.

The Warlord raised one hand—and the stone above cracked apart in a blinding explosion.

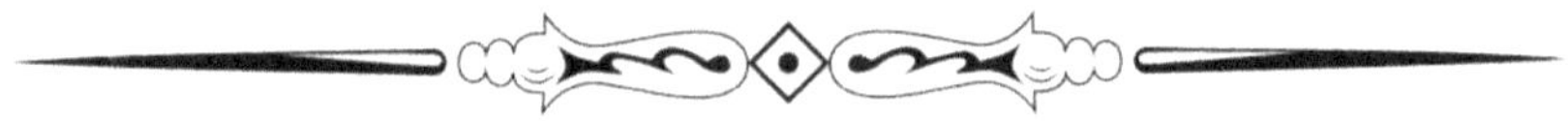

Elric grabbed his father with one arm, the wand held tight in the other. "Liora—guard us!"

She was already dashing, sword in one hand, sigil-stone in the other. "Go!"

They dashed toward the broken wall as fire and shadow clashed in battle behind them. The Tower screamed as if it knew its prey was fleeing.

The exit was narrow, decaying—barely a crawlspace. But it was an escape.

And behind them, the Warlord's voice thundered one last time, smooth and cold:

"You carry the Flame. The Plateau will never stop pursuing you."

Then the wall crumbled with a roar, blinding him from view.

The tunnel walls collapsed under pressure and heat as they retreated down the exit route, the air thick with ash and remembrance. Behind them, the Tower of Threads burned—a conflagration of stolen memories, melting into the shadows like abandoned whispers.

They broke through into daylight as the eastern horizon began to gray. There was smoke writhing up on the breeze into the high black fangs of the Plateau.

Calwen collapsed into Elric's arms, too tired to say anything, but living.

For the moment.

They set him down gently in the shelter of a broken outpost, shielded by the skeletons of stone once meant to deflect war.

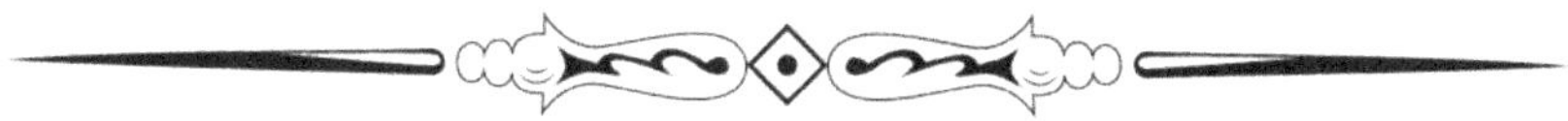

Elric dropped to his knees at his father's side, watching firelight play across his father's white face. The man was whole… but Elric was not. There was a feeling tugging at him—one of loss, unbearably strange. Like not recalling the words to a lullaby he'd sung a thousand times.

Liora's head fell, her shoulders heaving in exhaustion.

"Elric," she struggled, "do you know why you're here?

He blinked.

The sound of "Calwen" was hollow, echoing a bell that had been struck but now silenced. He knew this man had come a long way for him. Knew. But the string—the connection—had been severed.

"I—I don't know," he whispered in a voice barely above a crack.

"But it feels… right.”

Nib edged closer, small eyes shining with an ache he could not hide. "That Binder stole from you. Something precious."

Elric looked down at his shaking hands, hoping by sheer force of will, some memory could return to him.

Then Liora produced something from beneath her cloak—a small, leather-bound book, corners burned, the spine worn to threads. It felt like a hidden treasure.

"It's your father's diary," she said, placing it into his hands. "You and he used to write in it. Maybe. maybe it will jog your memory."

He took it up, his fingers knotting the cover of worn leather as if it were a sacred text.

The tower groaned behind them, a dying god of fire and mystery. The wind shrieked its ashes across the plain.

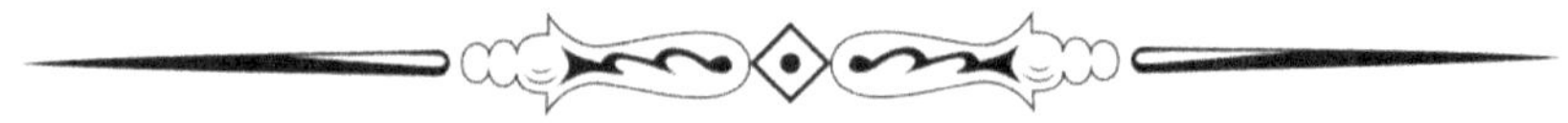

Elric opened the book—and on the first page, in slant, ink-spattered script, was a message from years gone by:

"For Elric. So, you'll always know where we started."

He traced the letters. Still nothing occurred.

But it stirred.

A warmth.

A flicker.

And Hope.

The wind howled across the Plateau, blowing away the tower's last ash into oblivion. Elric stood there, the book held out in his hand, his heart still burning with questions—and with lost purpose.

And though they had escaped the Tower.

Their journey was nowhere near over.

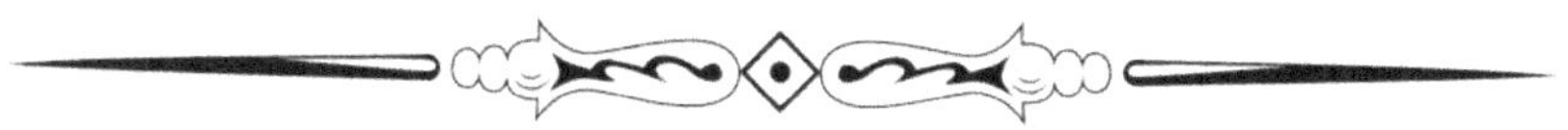

Chapter Thirteen
The Cost of Magic

The Tower of Threads burned in the distance, its flames flickering like the final light of a dying star with its last flicker of light.

They went quietly at first. The sort that clings like fog and makes every step weigh more heavily. Elric stepped with the journal concealed under his arm, as though it would anchor something he could no longer identify. His father—Calwen—moved cautiously, supported by Liora's shoulder, his frame still displaying the marks of the memory-weave.

"Are you sure you're alright?" Elric asked, his voice thin, searching. Not because he remembered the bond, but because his chest hurt, which meant that he should be.

Calwen smiled faintly. "I am now… though I wish you didn't have to suffer for it."

Elric blinked. "I don't understand."

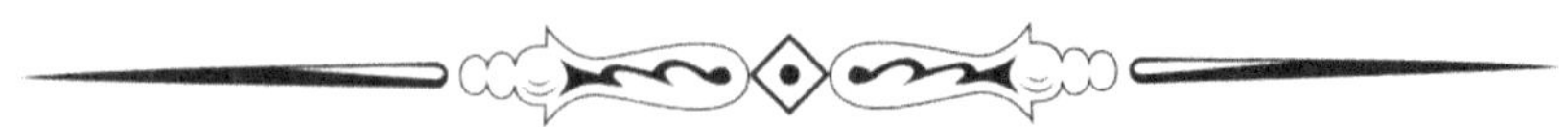

Nib, who had been trailing behind them, stopped chewing lazily on a blade of dry grass and cleared his throat.

"You gave up something strong," he said, his eyes lower than normal. "The last day you spent with your father before war broke out. That was… central magic. Cord-and-heart business."

Elric's eyes fell. The phrase felt like something overheard through beautiful glass, but distant.

Liora's gaze met hers once more. "We have to go. The Plateau warlords will not have the destruction of the tower go unanswered.".

They took shelter that night in a shattered windmill, its sails missing and its stone hull half-engulfed by vines. They crowded inside, close to a fire Elric summoned nearly without reflection. The flames flickered in odd colors—silver and purple, like the tower's yarns.

Liora curled beside him and gingerly opened the journal.

"Want me to read a bit?" she asked.

Elric nodded wordlessly.

Liora opened the cover with reverence, the little leather book trembling in her hands. Her voice was soft, hesitant, as if she were rousing a slumbering forest.

"Here," she said. "This one… this is you."

She cleared her throat and read in a loud voice:

"Today we caught two frogs, and Father asked me to name them both. He said a wizard always names his friends. I named the first one Sir Croaks-a-lot, and the second one. Pancake."

The silence that came after was thick. Elric didn't move. He didn't say a word, eyes scanned the ground, unfocused.

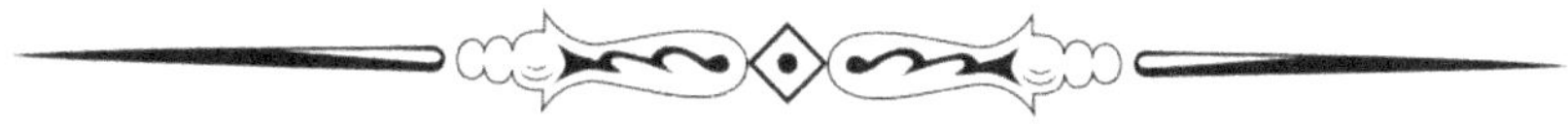

Then—his lip curled. A single, stunned breath of laughter escaped.

Liora looked up, hope lighting her face.

"I remember… the pond," Elric breathed. "It was at the back of our house. The reeds came up to my level, and he—he was always telling me I was half frog anyway."

He pressed a hand to his heart, as if steadying something fragile.

Nib snuffled from Elric's shoulder and grunted. "Pancake was a brave frog. Squishy, yes. And very, very slow."

Elric blinked over and over, and for the first time since the tower, his vision cleared.

Liora smiled. "You see? That's still you."

She turned the page and read more softly:

"Dad says someday I'll cast spells so wonderful the forest itself will dance. He believes in me, even when I stumble over my own boots."

A tear rolled down Elric's cheek—but he smiled.

"That was real. That was mine."

Liora closed the book gently. "Your memories are still there. Just… tangled in the threads. But they're not gone."

Behind them, the last of the tower's threads unraveled into the smoke-laced sky.

And though they didn't yet know where the road ahead would lead, something had been reclaimed. Not just a memory.

A reason.

Elric looked eastward, gripping the journal with steadier hands.

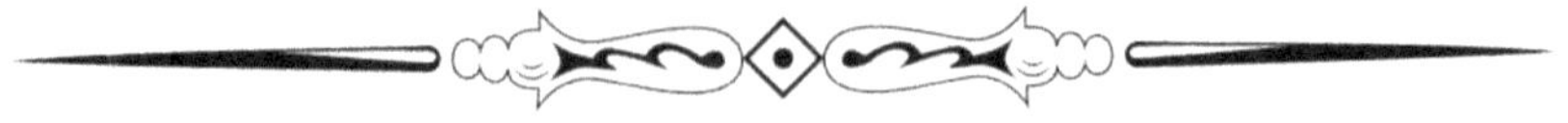

"I'm not done." silence fell.

Then, cautiously, Elric spoke, hesitantly. "I want to remember. I must. But it's like chasing mist. The nearer I get, the more it slips away from me."

Calwen shifted from where he had been lying, his gaze on them, though red-rimmed with fatigue.

"You're still you, Elric. Memory or not. And you came for me. "That means everything."

Elric flipped the journal about in his hands. It was warm, like a hearth at night in winter.

And then the flames danced higher.

Visages capered in the flames—fuzzy and dancing, yet true.

A running child across green fields, laughter spilling like winds. A lake, quiet and gray. A shadow on the ground from the trees. A summer voice, warm as sun.

Snippets only. But they pricked harder than reason—down into memory and soul and something older.

Suddenly, a low, bone-rasping snarl shredded the air outside.

Liora stood when the sound stopped. Nib snarled, fur bristling.

Past the destroyed windmill, out into the rolling fog, dark-armored figures coalesced. Glinting pale eyes glowed behind mirrored helms. They moved silently, chains trailing from their wrists that flashed and crackled with stolen magic—souls stitched into their lengths.

"The Threadhunters," Calwen croaked, spittle on his lips. "They sent their shadows."

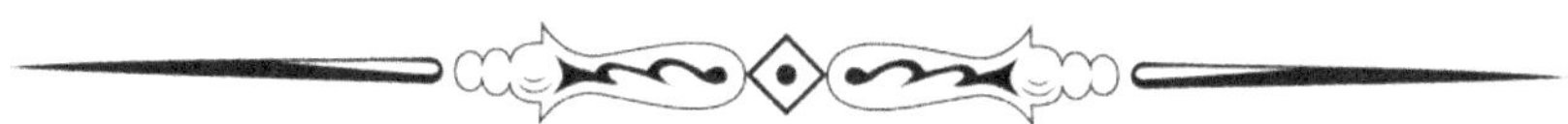

"We have to get out!" Liora bellowed, drawing her blade.

Slowly, Elric rose, the journal clutched tight in one hand—his bridge to an unretrievable self. In the other, his wand flared softly with fire, burning like a learning heartbeat.

He looked at his father.

At Liora.

At Nib.

And without knowing how he knew, only that he did, Elric said words that came from some hidden chamber of his heart.

The fires flared up, consuming them in a circle of living flame. The Threadhunters reversed, stumbling backward.

For one moment, the night hesitated in its breath.

Then they fled—into darkness, into darkness, into the unknown once more.

Behind them, from the dying echo of flame, a voice whispered through the smoke:

"Magic remembers even when you forget."

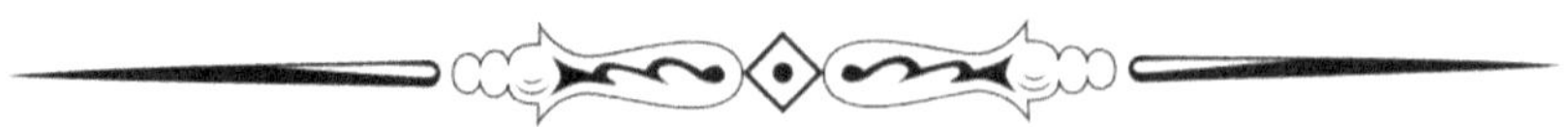

Chapter Fourteen

Return of the Whispering Forest

The trees leaned as if to listen. Their limbs curled overhead, unwound and susurrating, not with wind—but memory. With every step Elric took, he disturbed something beneath the moss, some buried awareness that rustled through the roots and rose into the leaves.

"This place," Liora whispered, "has been waiting."

Elric's wand throbbed, faintly, to the rhythm of the forest floor. A hush crept over them—not hush, but listening quiet, as if one held breath in anticipation.

Nib clung to Elric's collar. "It recalls you came back.".

As Elric crossed over the gnarled gate of the Whispering Forest, the wind swiveled.

It was no longer air—it carried scent and sound like patterned fabric: charred stone, salt tears, lullabies from far elder beings. The trees above

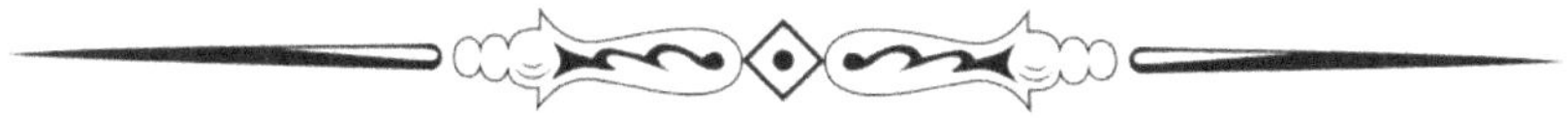

groaned not at chance, but purpose—reciting tales of his journey, of flame and mist, of broken spires and broken memory.

"Other now," Nib breathed, his own voice almost a whisper. He matched Elric's pace, his eyes lifted where leaves were darkened by rune-glow. "As if the trees… wait."

"They are," Liora told him, face impassive as she fitted an arrow into her bow. "And they recall."

A creaking groan seeped through the branches, like a desperate suck through old lungs. Somewhere deeper in the forest, a bark-skin drumbeat thudded—once, then again.

Elric's wand vibrated at his side.

"They're not merely remembering," he whispered.

"They're watching."

They moved in silence, the kind that grew with each step, as if the woods themselves enwrapped their minds. The trees grew stranger here.

Their trunks were inscribed with runes which glowed blue, pulsing in time with Elric's heart. Vines fell in ribbons from above, heavy with dew that glowed softly blue. The air thrummed—not with sound, but with something older than words. A hum. A knowledge.

Elric traversed over a root that coiled like a snake, and for a moment his foot slid into the moss—so soft it felt like touching memory itself. He caught snatches: his mother's song, his father's smile. The first time he'd ever seen fire dance out of his palms.

"This place." he whispered, "it remembers more than I do."

"Careful," Liora warned, gazing about them. "The forest doesn't only recall. It mirrors.".

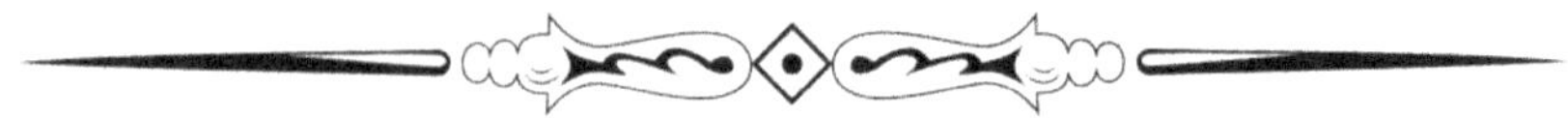

A tree in front of them creaked—not split or cracked but parted—revealing a hollow path within. Inside, the wood glowed with veins of gold, and the scent of rain and smoldering sage wafted out.

"Do we go through?" Nib asked, eyes wide with awe and terror.

Elric stepped forward, once nodding. "It's leading us. It knows where to go."

And they walked into the heartwood path.

The tree closed up behind them silently.

Calwen, pale and stricter now, stopped under a towering root-bridge. "Here you came into magic for the first time, didn't you?"

Elric nodded, but the memory stuck like mist—there, but shapeless. But as his boots sank into mossy soil, warmth seeped through him. Not fire, not sun—but something older. A sense of recognition. The forest did not recognize him as a stranger. It wrapped him round like a familiar cloak renewed.

Not a mere traveler. Not a mere boy.

Something it had molded to be.

The path curled like a creature, twisting in quiet and spilling past trees older than governments. Air vibrated with a distant light that was heavy with memory. Leaves whispered above not from wind, but from whisper—whispers of soft voices speaking names Elric had forgotten to have.

And then, from the green-glowing mist of the thicket, others emerged.

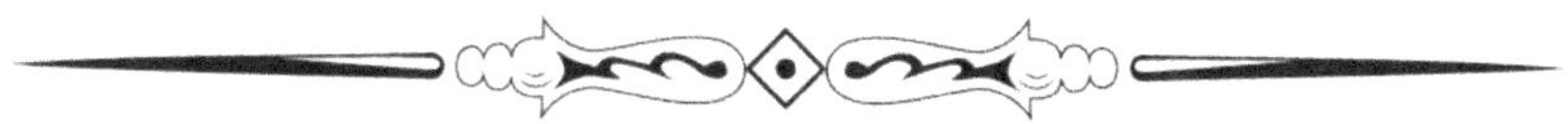

An owl descended in silence, wings trailing silver smoke, eyes aglow with the whisper of moonlight. It perched upon a bent branch and looked, then dipped its head in grave recognition.

A fox followed, its pelt etched with runes that beat with Elric's heart rhythm. It padded forward, circled him once, and lightly touched its tail against his knee—an old fellow, communicating in silence on recall.

And then the Will-o'-Whisps.

Scores, maybe scores more—winking sparks of blue fire that floated in from the trees, spinning in whirling orbits. Elric smiled, as they danced around him in the air, the way a man would smile remembering fairy tales on the eve of sleep.

"They know you," Liora breathed, bow lowered.

"Or they know the individual I used to be," Elric said softly, watching the lights trace the line of his wand.

Nib sniffed, respectfully for once. "This is like witnessing a tale walk."

They proceeded in silence, deeper and deeper, as the forest watched—not warily, but in hope. The trail ahead of them shone softly now, lit by bioluminescent roots and moss that parted to let them through.

And behind, the silhouettes vanished into the shadows once more—guardians of a remembrance not yet recalled in its entirety.

But soon.

Soon it would be.

"You sure you want to do this?" Liora asked quietly. "You could hold onto your magic. It is yours now. Nobody would condemn you."

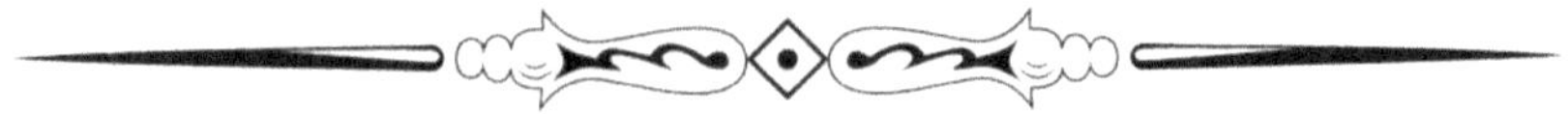

Elric did not answer at first.

They finally came to the Glade of First Light, where it had all begun. The clearing was ringed by weathered stones, and at its center pulsed a pool of light—a living remembrance of the forest's heart.

From the pool stepped the Forest Spirit, standing taller than ever before, its face both timeless and sorrowful.

Silence descended over the grove, deep as snow. Strands of light cut through the canopy in sloping beams, illuminating dust motes and entrapping them like stars. And centered was the Spirit—not tree nor beast, but some vast and rooted thing, shrouded in bark and shadow, eyes afire with the slow-burning patience of ages.

"Elric," it spoke, its voice groaning wood and snapping leaves. "You have come far. You have traded memory for sorcery, defied the Plateau, scorched the skies with runes made of woe. But nothing gratis is ever given. The land still aches under the weight of what was broken."

The forest in general drew its breath with it, all the trees leaning forth.

Elric stepped forward, wand weak in his hand. "Tell me what I must do."

The Spirit's limbs, contorted like branches that had been petrified, rose up slowly. Runes glimmered along its convoluted body—pain-wracked, ancient magic. It gestured toward the clearing around them, where saplings had sprouted in a circle, fragile, and trembling.

"You stand at a hinge in the world," it said. "You may keep what you've taken—your flame, your shellwork, the strength to shape wind, root, and fire. Build cities, break walls, cast back the shadow that hunts."

A pause, deep and painful.

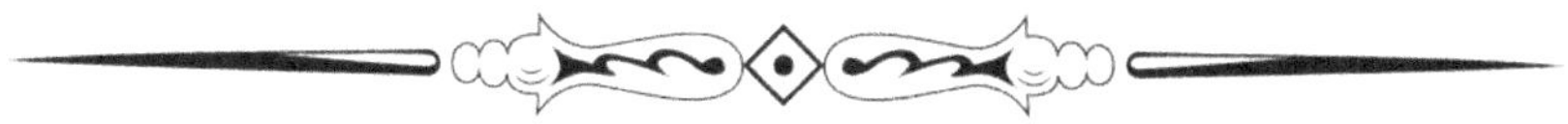

Or, the Spirit went on, its voice as low as concealed stone, "you can relinquish it. Heal the forest. Seal the fissure gouged by greed and war. Restore what was stilled—the river's song, the recollection of the roots, the souls laid to ash."

The air hesitated about Elric. Even the will-o'-whisps stopped their swirling dance.

The Spirit's eyes met his, deep and serious. "But in doing so, your power will wane. The runes will grow quiet. The whispers will cease. The fire within you will fade."

Liora's hand touched his shoulder. Nib dug deeper into his collar.

Elric looked down at his hand—thin scars drawn by glinting sigils, bought at the price of loss and longing. He could feel the fire-wand in his pack humming weakly not with order—but with question.

A gift or a curse?

Below, a breeze roamed through the foliage, carrying with it the sound of a lullaby—his mother's voice, distant and soft, as if the trees themselves remembered.

He closed his eyes. Nib sneezed. "I refuse that one, as well."

Liora did not speak, but merely looked at him with an expression edging toward respect.

Elric looked at his father, then at the journal in his cloak.

Inside, his past lay—though memory was a mist, stitched with ash and whispers. But something profound stirred now. Not memory but resolve. The truth is more absolute than names or faces.

"Looking for his father, a boy did," Elric whispered like rain. "But in searching him out... I found who I was to become."

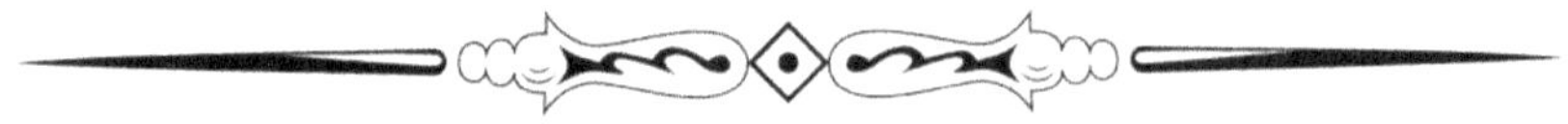

He emerged from darkness, stepping forward into the ring of light where moss burned emerald fire under his feet.

The wand at his hip stilled.

The runes on his arms broke away.

And the forest sang.

It sang in leaf-bells of wind, in the soft hush of branches folding low, in the soft thrum of roots remembering a name that mattered.

Elric.

Magic flowed from him in glistening filaments—gold and green, silver and blue—each thread weaving back into the world's rich tapestry. The trees shone. The sky brightened, a great breath of blue following a storm that had held the land for so long.

And within that instant, the fire of the war was extinguished in the east.

And so, the world was made whole.

The chain-magic binding the others ceased, shattering like glass with the echo of wind-swept bells ringing in the distance.

Elric dropped to his knees—but the woods seized him. Moss cushioned the fall. Illumination filtering through the leaves was soft.

When he opened his eyes, the Spirit disappeared. The patch of light stilled.

Nib wiped at a tear. "Well, you're still upright, and you're not a mushroom. Something to that effect."

Liora smiled wearily and sincerely. "The balance is restored. You did it."

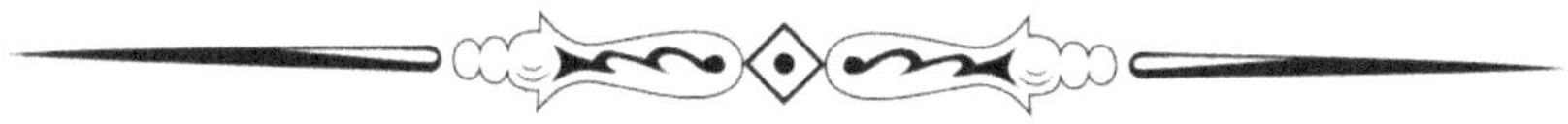

Calwen knelt beside him, eyes old with grief and newly calm. "You won't remember everything we shared, son. But I do. And I am proud—of the boy you once were, and the one you chose to become."

Elric gazed down at the journal in his lap. No fire leaped from his fingers now. No vines whispered. No rocks danced through the air.

But the forest remained with him—its tone gentle, its memory whole.

And that, he knew, was enough.

The four of them stepped out from under the last arms of the Whispering Forest into a world mending at last.

Not by power.

Not by magic.

But by hope.

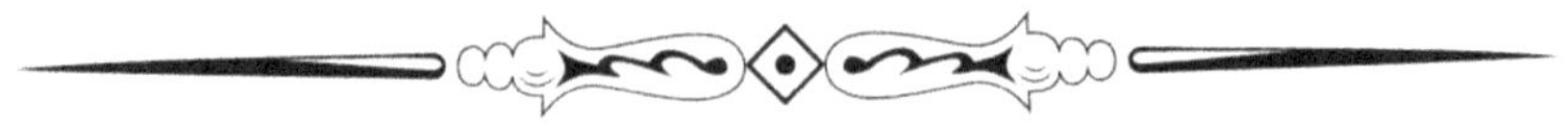

Epilogue
The Forest Remembers

Seasons passed.

The Eastern Plateau's hold slipped away like melting ice. Deprived of stolen magic from others to support their cruel domination, the warlords dissolved into myths—scattered and forgotten. A peace, fragile and tentative, bloomed in the emptiness between ash.

And in the heart of the world, the Whispering Forest bloomed greener than ever.

They inform you that occasionally—when the moonlight bends just so—you can still hear the sound of a boy's laughter echoing through the trees. A reminder that magic does not live in spells or sparks, but in the choices, we make.

Particularly, the hard ones.

A fresh tree grew in the First Light Glade. It bore no fruit, but its bark radiated softly with the gentle glow of old memories. Children sat

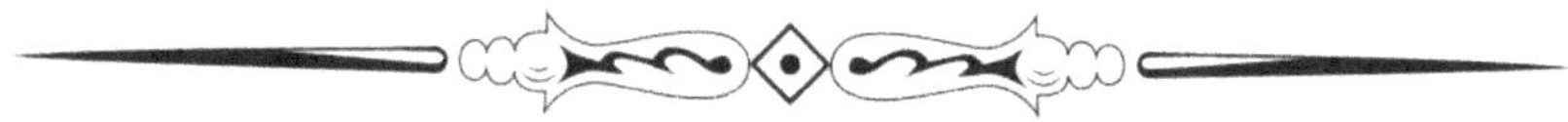

beneath its sprawling shadow and listened as the forest whispered stories to them. There was one that always returned:

The boy who returned what he could not hold, to preserve what he could not let go.

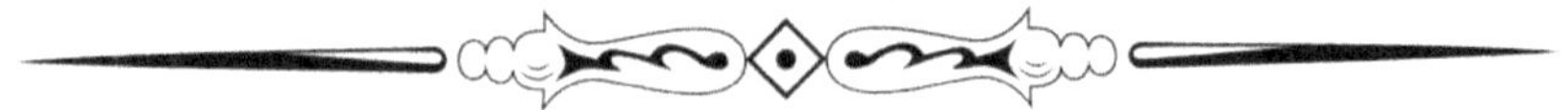